GRAY

TRUTH OF LIFE

PREETI KHANKHOJE

Made with ♥ on the Notion Press Platform
www.notionpress.com

Contents

"Life's truth lies in the shades of gray, where complexities unfold and perceptions sway."

"Amidst the gray, truth finds its way, shaping our choices and guiding our stay."

-Preeti Khankhoje

Author's Note

Life is a complex tapestry of shades of gray, where the lines between right and wrong can blur and perspectives differ. What may be the right choice for one person may not hold true for another. It is crucial to remember that differing opinions or actions don't necessarily make someone wrong. Situations shape our thoughts and reactions, influencing our perception of what is best.

In the midst of uncertainty, it is important to extend the benefit of doubt and avoid hasty judgments. Instead, seek understanding through open communication and thoughtful consideration. Taking the time to talk things out and weigh the potential outcomes can lead to finding the best possible solution.

Embrace the freedom to do what feels comfortable and appropriate for you, without being solely governed by the fear of consequences. Trust your instincts and make choices that align with your values and aspirations. Remember that the judgments we pass on others should be based not only on their actions but also on their intentions. Taking this holistic approach allows for greater empathy and understanding.

In the tapestry of life, family is an invaluable thread that weaves us together. Stand by your family, defending their well-being and nurturing the bonds that hold you close. Even in the midst of adversity, cling to the belief that family is everything. Trust in the strength of your shared love and stand united, finding solace and courage in each other's presence.

Above all, prioritize your own happiness and follow the desires of your heart. Forge your own path, make decisions that align with your innermost beliefs, unburdened by the expectations of others. Stand firmly alongside your loved ones, offering support and fighting for what you believe in. Even in the face of challenging circumstances, hold steadfast to your values, knowing that they will guide you towards the right course of action.

I am deeply grateful to my husband, my first reader, for his belief in my stories and plots. I am immensely grateful to my extraordinary daughter for her persistent support and encouragement throughout this journey. Her unwavering belief in me and my abilities has been a constant source of inspiration and motivation. Her infectious enthusiasm has brought joy to every step of this endeavour. Their love and support have been truly invaluable. I must also express my heartfelt appreciation to my sisters, who have been a constant source of laughter, joy, and firm belief in my abilities. Their encouragement to explore new horizons has made this journey all the more fulfilling. I am profoundly fortunate to have such an exceptional support system, and I will forever cherish your presence in my life. Their insights and perspectives have been instrumental in refining and enhancing the final version of this book.

This book is dedicated to all the strong women who have the power to accomplish anything, who tirelessly support their families, and who fearlessly follow their hearts, carving their own path. Your strength and determination inspire me, and it is my hope that this book resonates with your spirit and empowers you on your own journey.

ONE

Heritage Unveiled

Winter 2005

On a winter morning in Delhi, the city had a peaceful and beautiful atmosphere. As the sun began to rise, the sky adorned itself with hues of soft pinks, golden yellows, and pale blues, creating a breath-taking backdrop for the city's awakening. The morning mist gently hung over the city, casting an enchanting veil over the landscape, blurring the edges of buildings and trees. As the first rays of sunlight broke through the mist, they cast a warm and golden glow upon the city's landmarks. Monuments and historical structures stood with stoic elegance, their architectural splendour accentuated by the soft light. The iconic Red Fort and Jama Masjid, shrouded in a delicate mist, exuded an aura of timeless grandeur. The streets of Delhi were quieter than usual in the early morning hours, as the city slowly stirred from its slumber. The sound of distant footsteps and occasional bicycle bells resonated through the air, creating a tranquil symphony that blended with the gentle rustling of leaves.

The winter foliage added colour to the surroundings. The parks and gardens had trees with leaves in shades of brown, gold, and amber, preparing for their fall. Dewdrops glistened like tiny diamonds on blades of grass, capturing the ethereal beauty of the morning.

In the heart of bustling Delhi, where life is full of energy and enthusiasm, there is a house that is vibrant, glamorous, and embodies the charm of a typical Delhi family. It is a place filled with activity, laughter, lively conversations, and a constant flow of visitors. This house is a perfect blend of tradition and modernity, where love and togetherness are at the core of its existence.

In this lively home, where love and togetherness are the most important, Riya, the cherished darling of her family, peacefully sleeps in her room. She is like an angel to her mother. As the soft morning light gently peeks through the curtains, kissing Riya's cheeks with its warm glow, the room comes alive as if touched by the magic of a new day. With a sweet smile on her lips, Riya stirs beneath her cozy blankets, feeling excited for the adventures that await her. The crisp morning air carries a whisper of anticipation, revealing the secrets and wonders that lie just beyond her dreams' doorstep.

Determined to embrace the day with boundless joy, she gracefully slips out of the realm of slumber and into the embrace of reality. Each step she takes is filled with a quiet confidence, her spirit alight with an infectious enthusiasm. As she emerges from the snug cocoon of her blankets, she selects her attire with tender care, knowing that each garment she chooses will not only shield her from the wintry chill but also become an expression of her vibrant personality. Layer by layer, she adorns herself with love, transforming her clothing into a canvas that mirrors her radiant spirit.

With sparkling eyes and an illuminating smile, Riya steps into the warm embrace of her home. Her heart dances with anticipation as she meets her mother, the embodiment of love and affection. Her mother's comforting smile radiates warmth, enveloping Riya like a soothing balm. In an instant, Riya rushes into her mother's waiting arms, finding solace and security. Wrapped in an embrace that speaks volumes, she lingers, savouring the comfort of her mother's presence and inhaling the familiar scent that fills her with a sense of belonging.

Next, Riya's eyes meet her father, who stands tall with a blend of pride and tenderness in his gaze. It's a look that speaks volumes of unconditional love and support. Riya walks toward him, her heart filled with gratitude for the constant support he has provided. As she stands before him, he reaches out and embraces her, his touch conveying both strength and tenderness, symbolizing his love and protective nature. In that sacred moment, she feels an invisible shield of love enveloping her, empowering her to face the day with utmost confidence.

In this lively home, where every soul is touched by Riya's presence, she carries with her an enchanting aura—a touch of magic that infuses every corner with joy, and a smile that lights up the room. After receiving blessings from her parents, Riya moves forward to greet the other members of her family. They gather around the table, their faces adorned with smiles, and their voices filled with warmth. The morning air is filled with the aroma of brewing tea, creating a sense of comfort and familiarity.

Riya takes her seat, her hands cupping the steaming mug of tea, letting its warmth seep into her fingertips. Soon, Riya's uncle and aunt, along with their cousins, Karan, Simran, and Anita, arrive with a basket of delicious treats in hand. They hand over the basket to Riya's mother, who graciously accepts it, appreciating the effort and love put into preparing the delectable dishes.

As everyone settles in, the cousins eagerly catch up,

sharing stories and laughter, while Riya's brother, Parminder, playfully teases Karan about a recent prank they pulled together. The gathering grows livelier with the addition of more laughter and camaraderie. Riya engages in lively conversations with her family, exchanging stories and laughter. They discuss the day ahead, sharing their plans and aspirations, and pondering over the possibilities that await them.

The room echoes with the clinking of spoons against teacups and the soft murmur of their voices. As they chat and share their thoughts, they also discuss the mouth-watering options for lunch, contemplating various delicacies that will tantalize their taste buds. They exchange suggestions and ideas, their excitement evident as they anticipate the flavours that will grace their plates.

Riya's college schedule demanded an early start, and she needed to be ready on time. She joins her family for a quick breakfast, savouring the hot tea and delicious homemade fare. The dining table is adorned with various dishes, ranging from steaming parathas to piping hot vegetable curries, halwa, milk and fruits providing nourishment and comfort for the day ahead. After bidding her family farewell, Riya makes her way to the bustling streets of Delhi. The city had come alive with activity, as commuters hurriedly made their way to work or educational institutions. Buses and auto-rickshaws honked their horns, vying for space on the busy roads, while pedestrians navigated the crowded sidewalks.

In the heart of Delhi, the college campus is bustling with excitement. Students from different disciplines gather, filling the air with lively conversations and laughter. Riya walks through the vibrant corridors, holding her textbooks tightly. She immerses herself in the stimulating atmosphere, ready to participate in lectures, discussions, and the pursuit of knowledge. In class, Riya becomes fully engaged in the enriching academic environment. The winter chill fades away as she focuses on her studies, exchanging ideas with classmates, and gaining inspiration from her professors. Each lecture brings a fresh perspective, expanding her horizons and shaping her understanding of the world.

Meanwhile, in Riya's family home, her mother is busy in the kitchen, orchestrating a symphony of flavours and aromas. The enticing spices fill the air as she skilfully prepares a delicious feast for the family. With each chop and stir, she infuses love and passion into every dish, creating a culinary masterpiece for the upcoming meal. While her mother works her magic in the kitchen, father and brother venture out to their showroom, a hub of activity and creativity. As they step into the bustling world of their family business, they immerse themselves in the dynamic realm of trade and commerce. Their mornings are filled with a whirlwind of phone calls, where they engage in discussions with clients, negotiate deals, and address any concerns or inquiries that arise.

Parminder, Riya's brother and father, Balminder share a remarkable bond that extends beyond their professional collaboration. Their relationship is built on respect, trust, and wisdom, which influences every aspect of their lives. Their strong sense of community and shared family values are evident in their actions and interactions with each other and the extended family. In the realm of their working department, Parminder and his father exhibit a deep understanding and appreciation for each other's roles and contributions. They have established clear divisions of labour, with Parminder overseeing tie-ups, marketing, and client meetings, while his father takes charge of accounts and administration. Their well-defined responsibilities allow them to work cohesively and efficiently, leveraging their individual strengths for the betterment of the business.

The foundation of their collaboration lies in open communication and mutual respect. They engage in frequent discussions, brainstorming sessions, and decision-making processes, valuing each person's opinions and insights. Parminder looks up to his father as a mentor and guide, seeking his wisdom and advice in both business and family matters. His father, in turn, takes pride in Parminder's growth and accomplishments, offering guidance and support to help him navigate the complexities of work and life. Beyond their professional sphere, Parminder and his father foster a sense of togetherness and belonging within the family. They recognize the importance of family values, traditions, and the overall well-being of each family member. They actively participate in family activities, celebrations, and rituals, instilling a strong sense of community and unity among all.

Parminder's love for his sister, Riya, is unconditional. He goes above and beyond to fulfill her wishes and support her dreams. Whether it's providing a thoughtful gift, organizing special outings, or being there for her during challenging times, or emotional guidance, being her confidant, or making efforts to bring a smile to her face, Parminder demonstrates his deep commitment to his sister's happiness and well-being. Their bond strengthens the sense of community within the family, creating an environment where love, support, and understanding thrive.

Balminder and his wife, Khushboo, as loving parents, extend their values of compassion, empathy, and understanding to their children, Riya and Parminder. They create a nurturing environment where their children feel supported, loved, and encouraged to grow into compassionate individuals. For example, when Riya comes home from school days feeling upset about a disagreement with her friend, Balminder and Khushboo actively listen to her concerns without judgment. They provide a safe space for her to express her feelings and thoughts. Instead of immediately offering solutions, they empathize with Riya's emotions and encourage her to explore different perspectives. Through this dialogue, Balminder and Khushboo help Riya develop her own problem-solving skills and find a resolution that promotes empathy and understanding.

In another instance, Parminder expresses an interest in helping people in need after watching a documentary about homelessness. Balminder and Khushboo seize this opportunity to cultivate his compassion. They engage in a family discussion, encouraging Parminder to share his thoughts and feelings about the issue. Together, they research local charitable organizations and participate as a family in volunteering or fundraising efforts to support the homeless community. Balminder and Khushboo's active involvement and support empower Parminder to take meaningful action, instilling in him a sense of empathy and a desire to make a positive difference.

Balminder and Khushboo also prioritize teaching their children the importance of gratitude and appreciation. During family dinners, they take turns sharing something they are grateful for, fostering a sense of gratitude in Riya and Parminder. Balminder and Khushboo lead by example, expressing gratitude for both big and small things in their own lives. This practice helps their children develop a mindset of appreciation and recognize the value of acknowledging the blessings and kindness they receive from others.

Moreover, Balminder and Khushboo encourage Riya and Parminder to embrace diversity and respect individuals from different backgrounds. They expose their children to diverse cultures through books, movies, and community events. They engage in conversations about different traditions, beliefs, and experiences, promoting understanding and acceptance. By encouraging Riya and Parminder to ask questions and engage in open discussions, Balminder and Khushboo foster a curiosity and appreciation for the richness of diversity in the world.

When conflicts arise between Riya and Parminder, Balminder and Khushboo teach their children constructive conflict resolution. They guide them through active listening, encouraging each child to express their feelings and concerns. Balminder and Khushboo emphasize the importance of understanding the other person's perspective and finding a compromise that respects both parties' needs. Through these experiences, Riya and Parminder learn to navigate conflicts with empathy and respect, building strong communication skills and cultivating harmonious relationships. By consistently demonstrating compassion, empathy, and understanding in their interactions with their children and others, Balminder and Khushboo create an environment where these values are deeply ingrained and understanding that extends beyond their immediate family and into the world around them.

Throughout the winter morning, Riya's family home is a hub of continuous activity. Relatives and friends visit, adding to the vibrant chaos that echoes through the halls. Laughter, animated conversations, and occasional disagreements create a dynamic atmosphere that characterizes the warmth and togetherness of Riya's family. As the day unfolds, Riya focuses on her studies, while her family attends to their respective responsibilities. The evenings are dedicated to quality time, where stories, laughter, and heartfelt conversations are shared, creating treasured moments that are etched in their hearts and with delicious food. When night falls, Riya finds peace in her room, reflecting on the day before preparing for a restful sleep. The house gradually settles into a serene silence, ready to embrace the tranquillity of the night and welcome another beautiful day together.

In bustling Chandni Chowk, there is a lively lane where Riya's family resides and operates their proud and bustling showroom. As you step into the vibrant lane of Chandni Chowk, your senses come alive with the symphony of sounds and sights that surround you. The air is filled with the constant chatter of pedestrians, shopkeepers, and rickshaw pullers, creating a lively ambiance that immerses you in the bustling energy of the place. On both sides of the lane, small shops adorned with colourful fabrics and beautifully crafted garments invite you to discover their treasures. The shopkeepers, eager to assist, greet you with warm smiles, invites you to discover and explore their exquisite offerings, enticing you with their best prices. The air is filled with the cheerful buzz of bargaining and haggling, creating a lively atmosphere as buyers and sellers engage in friendly negotiations, adding an exciting and dynamic vibe to the scene the latest fashion trends and engage in the art of negotiation. The hustle and bustle of rickshaws and cycle-rickshaws weaving through the traffic, accompanied by the melodic chime of their bells, add to the energetic atmosphere. Occasionally, the lane comes alive with the passing of a wedding procession, accompanied by drummers and musicians who fill the air with joyous tunes, heightening the festive spirit.

The charm of Chandni Chowk lies not only in its lively commerce but also in its architectural splendour. The buildings that line the lane bear the marks of time, with ornate balconies, intricate carvings, and wooden frames that tell stories of a bygone era. As you navigate through the bustling lane, your senses are further tantalized by the delightful aromas wafting through the air. The fragrance of freshly brewed tea from nearby chai stalls mingles with the alluring spices of street food vendors, tempting you to indulge in samosas, parathas, jalebis, and chaat. The sizzling sounds and mouth-watering smells create an irresistible invitation to taste the culinary delights offered in this vibrant lane.

Riya's family's showroom, located in the bustling Chandni Chowk area of Delhi, stands as a proud symbol of his family's legacy and expertise in the garment industry. The showroom's signboard proudly displays their family name, *(Malhotra's Garments Since 1928)* indicating a long-standing tradition of providing high-quality garments to the community. Upon entering the showroom, one is greeted by a vibrant display of colourful fabrics that catch the eye. The racks are adorned with a wide range of garments, including sarees, salwar suits, lehengas, jewellery, accessories and other traditional Indian attire. Each piece is carefully chosen for its craftsmanship, design, and attention to detail.

Mannequins positioned strategically throughout the showroom showcase the latest fashion trends and designs, giving customers a visual representation of how the garments look when worn, highlighting the elegance and beauty of the traditional attire available at *Malhotra's Garments*. As customers step into showroom, they are immediately enveloped in an atmosphere of warmth and genuine hospitality. The showroom is more than just a place to shop; it is a haven where customers are treated like cherished guests. The family's commitment to providing an exceptional shopping experience begins with a heartfelt welcome. As the doorbell chimes, friendly smiles and warm greetings await every visitor.

Balminder and his wife Khushboo, an expert in the art of hospitality, take center stage in delighting the customers. With her culinary expertise, she prepares a delightful array of freshly brewed teas and snacks each infused with her secret blend of aromatic spices. As customers sip on their tea, Balminder, Parminder engage in genuine conversations, eager to know more about their visitors. They take the time to understand each customer's preferences, style, and requirements, tailoring the shopping experience to cater to individual needs. Whether a customer is seeking a traditional outfit for a special occasion or a trendy ensemble for everyday wear, Balminder and Parminder shares their wealth of knowledge about traditional garments, fabrics, and fashion trends. Their genuine passion for their craft shines through, leaving customers enthralled and confident in their choices.

Beyond just guiding customers through the racks of garments, Balminder and Parminder goes the extra mile to make each visit truly memorable. They offer personalized styling tips, suggesting accessories that complement the chosen outfits. The showroom is adorned with mirrors and a comfortable seating area, allowing customers to try on outfits at their leisure while receiving compliments and encouragement from the family. But that's not all, Balminder and Parminder understands the importance of making every customer feel pampered and special. In the showroom, they have dedicated lounges for brides-to-be to relax, sip on refreshments, and enjoy a moment of comfort. Additionally, a luxurious bridal room awaits, equipped with full-length mirrors and elegant dressing tables for personalized consultations with expert stylists, ensuring perfection for their special day. To express their gratitude to loyal customers and create a sense of belonging, Balminder and Parminder have introduced a unique royalty program. This exclusive program rewards customers with special privileges, such as early access to new collections, personalized styling sessions, and invitations to exclusive fashion events.

Balminder and Parminder meticulously wrap every

purchase like a beautifully crafted gift, adding a handwritten thank-you note to show their appreciation and make customers feel special. They also host occasional fashion workshops and cultural events, fostering a sense of community and allowing customers to embrace traditional garments' rich heritage.

Riya's ancestral house is also in Chandni Chowk, known as *'The Malhotra's'*, stands as a magnificent embodiment of grandeur and architectural beauty. Nestled amidst the bustling lanes, this house serves as a resolute guardian of history, preserving the essence of Delhi's rich cultural heritage. It's a 2-floor house with gardens on both sides and a terrace. Elaborately designed and meticulously maintained, Malhotra's House exudes an aura of timeless elegance that captivates all who set foot inside. As one approaches the house, they are greeted by an ornate entrance gate that opens into a serene courtyard, a rare oasis of tranquillity amidst the chaotic city. The courtyard is a sight to behold, adorned with intricate marble carvings featuring delicate floral patterns and motifs, a testament to the craftsmanship of a bygone era. At its center stands a mesmerizing marble fountain, its gentle gurgling providing a soothing soundtrack to the surroundings. The house's facade boasts intricately carved sandstone, showcasing exquisite details depicting mythological scenes and geometric patterns that inspire a sense of wonder. Every room within Malhotra's House is meticulously designed, reflecting a perfect blend of traditional elegance and modern comforts.

Riya's journey through her law college years was enriched by her close-knit group of friends, who accompanied her through the ups and downs of her studies and personal growth. Together, they formed a supportive and vibrant community within the realm of their law college. Riya's friendship circle consisted of a diverse group of individuals, each with their unique personalities and strengths. Some were passionate debaters, always ready for intellectual discussions, while others were compassionate listeners, offering a comforting ear during challenging times. Together, they formed a cohesive unit that uplifted and inspired one another.

Law college demanded rigorous academic engagement, and Riya and her friends would often come together for study sessions. They would gather in the library or find a cozy corner in a nearby café, armed with their textbooks, highlighters, and coffee. Collaboratively, they would tackle complex legal concepts, share study materials, and engage in stimulating discussions, fostering a supportive and conducive learning environment. One of the highlights of Riya's law college experience was participating in moot court competitions. Riya and her friends would prepare meticulously, honing their advocacy skills and crafting persuasive arguments. They would spend hours practicing mock trials, helping each other refine their presentation styles and addressing potential counterarguments. The camaraderie and healthy competition among friends added an extra layer of excitement and motivation to their preparation.

Beyond the academic realm, Riya and her friends would actively participate in extracurricular activities organized by the law college. They would form teams for quizzes, debates, and cultural events, showcasing their talents and fostering a sense of camaraderie among fellow students. These activities offered a platform for self-expression, personal growth, and the cultivation of well-rounded personalities.

Riya and her friends understood the importance of balancing academics with leisure. They would plan outings to explore the city, visit historical sites, or simply unwind in local cafes. They were cautious and careful about the timing of returning home. As they all stayed nearby to each other, they usually planned their evenings at a nearby café, as Delhi after 8 PM was generally considered risky for girls.These social gatherings provided a much-needed break from the demanding academic schedule, allowing them to bond, create cherished memories, and strengthen their friendships outside the confines of the law college. Riya's friends served as her pillars of support during challenging times. Whether it was navigating demanding coursework, dealing with exam stress, or managing personal issues, they were there to lend a listening ear, provide guidance, and offer words of encouragement.

As graduation approached, Riya and her friends celebrated their accomplishments with pride and joy. They marked this milestone with laughter, tears, and promises to stay connected in their future endeavours. Even as they embarked on different paths, they remained a tight-knit group, supporting and inspiring each other as they ventured into the legal profession. Riya's friends in law college played an integral role in shaping her personal and professional growth. Their camaraderie, shared experiences, and mutual support contributed to a vibrant and fulfilling college life.

TWO

A Passionate Pursuit

During her final year of college, Riya found herself drawn to her family's business. In her free time, she would often visit the showroom, observing the intricate details of the operations and immersing herself in the world of fashion and retail. The sight of vibrant garments, beautifully displayed accessories, and the bustling energy of the showroom fascinated her. It was during one sunny afternoon, while Riya was engrossed in the showroom, that a sudden spark of inspiration ignited within her. As she interacted with the customers, witnessed the seamless coordination between the sales team, and admired the craftsmanship of the products, Riya couldn't help but feel a deep sense of admiration for the business her family had built. The dedication and passion that permeated every aspect of the operation resonated with her own aspirations. She recognized the potential to contribute to the growth and success of the business, and the thought of playing a role in its development excited her.

It was as if a light bulb had switched on in her mind, illuminating a brilliant idea. Riya realized that her knowledge and skills from business law studies could be put to good use in furthering the family business. She saw an opportunity to blend her passion for entrepreneurship with her love for fashion and retail. The idea of actively participating in the decision-making process, strategizing for growth, and exploring innovative avenues for expansion sparked a renewed sense of purpose within her. Riya's visits to the showroom became more frequent, and she eagerly absorbed every aspect of the business, from inventory management to customer relations. She sought guidance from her parents, asking questions about their experiences, challenges they had faced, and the vision they had for the future. Her family, recognizing her genuine interest and dedication, welcomed her with open arms, providing mentorship and support as she explored her newfound passion.

As Riya continued her studies, she couldn't help but envision a future where she would play an active role in taking the family business to new heights. The showroom became a place of inspiration and learning, where she honed her business acumen and developed a deeper understanding of the industry. With each passing day, her belief in the potential of the business and her own capabilities grew stronger. As the years passed by, Riya found herself excelling in both her legal career at the prestigious law firm in Delhi and her responsibilities in the family business. Balancing her legal practice on weekdays and managing the showroom on weekends, she embraced the dual roles with unwavering determination and passion. Riya's dedication and hard work were evident as she poured her heart into both endeavour's, leaving a mark of excellence in every task she undertook. Her ability to manage multiple responsibilities with finesse and dedication earned her admiration from her colleagues and family alike.

One sunny afternoon, while Riya was engrossed in her work, she suddenly remembered that her dear college friend's birthday was approaching. Her friend had recently embarked on a new chapter of her life in Mumbai, pursuing a career at a prestigious News Channel. As Riya reminisced about the countless memories they had shared during their college days, a wave of nostalgia washed over her. Riya's heart overflowed with joy as she began meticulously planning the surprise. She wanted everything to be perfect, just like their college days. She reached out to their mutual friends, sharing her idea and rallying their support. Together, they brainstormed and devised a plan that would ensure a truly unforgettable experience for their dear friend. With each passing day, Riya's anticipation mounted. With great care and thoughtfulness, she curated a special gift designed to bring a heartfelt smile to her friend's face. Additionally, she rallied their college friends, encouraging them to send personalized messages and heartfelt video greetings. Together, they created a beautiful birthday tribute that reflected their cherished shared history, evoking fond memories of their college days.

In the days that followed, Riya eagerly counted down to the birthday surprise. She diligently packed her bags, booked the tickets, and reserved a cozy hotel, ensuring that every detail was taken care of. She imagined the joyous reunion, the laughter, the tears of happiness, and the heartfelt conversations that awaited them in the vibrant city by the sea. As Riya's flight touched down in Mumbai, she felt a sense of exhilaration and nervousness. She took a deep breath, collected her belongings, and made her way through the bustling airport. The city's vibrant atmosphere welcomed her with open arms, igniting a sense of adventure and celebration. On the day of her friend's birthday, Riya carefully coordinated with her friend's and colleagues to ensure that everything fell into place.

With the birthday gift carefully wrapped and held tightly in her hand, Riya arrived at the bustling News Channel where her friend Vidya now worked. The excitement within her was palpable as she made her way through the familiar corridors, navigating the maze of busy journalists and buzzing newsrooms. As Riya reached Vidya's office, she paused to collect her thoughts, her heart pounding with anticipation. Taking a deep breath, she gently opened the door, and there stood Vidya, fully engrossed in her work. As Vidya looked up, her eyes widened in disbelief and delight at the sight of Riya standing at the doorway, a radiant smile gracing her face. Time seemed to stand still as their gazes locked, a mixture of surprise, joy, and disbelief mirrored in their eyes. Overwhelmed by the rush of emotions, Vidya could do nothing but rush forward and embrace Riya in a tight, heartfelt hug. No words were needed in that moment, as their eyes met, conveying a profound appreciation and understanding of their unbreakable bond. It was a wordless exchange, filled with unspoken gratitude, admiration, and an sense of value for the special connection they shared. After a few precious moments, Riya gently pulled away and presented the carefully chosen birthday gift to Vidya.

Riya: "Happy birthday, Vidya! I hope this gift brings you as much joy as your friendship brings to my life."

Vidya: (With a smile) "Oh, Riya, you shouldn't have! I can't wait to see what's inside."

Riya: "I put a lot of thought into it. I hope you'll love it."

Vidya: (After unwrapping the gift) "Wow, Riya! This is absolutely amazing! Thank you so much. You really know how to make a someone feel special."

Riya: "You deserve all the love and surprises today, Vidya. But there's more to come. Are you ready for another surprise?"

Vidya: (Curiously) "Another surprise? You've already made my day so special. I can't imagine what else you have in store."

Riya: "Well, I have a one more plan for your birthday. I've arranged a surprise celebration for you at one of the most charming restaurants in town."

Vidya: (Excitedly) "A surprise celebration? That sounds fantastic! But how did you manage all of this?"

Riya: "Oh, you know me – I'm a master planner! I reached out to our college friends and your friends here in Mumbai too and ensured that they'll be there to celebrate with us."

Vidya: (Touched) "Riya, you're incredible! Thank you for going above and beyond to make this day so memorable."

Riya: "Anything for you, Vidya. You're not just a friend; you're family to me. And I wanted to make your birthday extra special, surrounded by all the people who care about you."

Vidya: "I'm truly blessed to have you in my life. This surprise celebration means the world to me."

Riya: "I'm thrilled that you're happy. Now, let's get ready for an unforgettable evening filled with laughter, joy, and lots of fun!"

Vidya: "I can't wait! Thank you, Riya, for being the best friend a person could ask for."

Riya: "Happy birthday, Vidya! Let's make this day one to remember!"

The restaurant was adorned with vibrant balloons, shimmering decorations, and a table brimming with delightful treats. As Vidya entered the space, she was greeted by a chorus of joyful voices and beaming smiles. The sheer magnitude of Riya's surprise left her momentarily speechless, her heart overflowing with gratitude. Laughter filled the air as Vidya's friends surrounded her, showering her with warmth and affection. The room was alive with the energy of their friendship, as they shared stories, reminisced about their college days, and created new memories together. Around the table, heartfelt conversations flourished, with each friend expressing their admiration for Vidya's compassion, intelligence, and support. The atmosphere was infused with a sense of gratitude for the beautiful soul that Vidya embodied and the impact she had on their lives. In that intimate setting, Vidya felt an overwhelming sense of love and appreciation for the incredible people surrounding her. The surprise celebration became a testament to the power of their friendship, a reminder of the support and the deep value they found in each other. They danced and sang all night, toasting to a better future, stronger bonds, and brighter years ahead. With a group hug, they bid farewell to the celebration. The next day, as Riya had a flight to catch, Vidya dropped her off at a hotel close to the airport.

Amidst of birthday celebration, Riya had the pleasure of meeting someone truly charming who happened to be a Vidya's friend. As the birthday celebration unfolded, Riya's eyes were drawn to this charismatic individual who effortlessly commanded attention. They had an air of confidence, a warm smile, and engaging conversation skills that instantly captivated Riya. Their presence in the group added a new dynamic, and Riya found herself intrigued by their charm and charisma.

Throughout the evening, Riya and the charming person engaged in deep and meaningful conversations. They shared stories, exchanged thoughts on various topics, and discovered common interests. Their discussions flowed effortlessly, as if they had known each other for a long time. Riya found herself drawn to their intelligence, wit, and the way they genuinely listened and connected with others. As the evening progressed, Riya and the charming person found themselves gravitating towards each other. They shared moments of laughter, shared glances filled with unspoken understanding, and even indulged in playful banter. Their connection felt natural and effortless, creating a sense of familiarity and warmth that was hard to ignore.

Although Riya and the charming person hadn't known each other for long, there was an undeniable chemistry between them. They shared stolen glances and exchanged subtle gestures that conveyed a deeper connection. Riya's heart fluttered in their presence, and she couldn't help but wonder if this chance meeting was something more than just a casual encounter. As Riya's celebration came to an end, bidding farewell to the charming person was bittersweet. They exchanged contact information, promising to keep in touch and explore the possibility of meeting again. Riya couldn't shake off the feeling that this encounter had left a lasting impression on her life, and she looked forward to seeing where this newfound connection might lead.

After returning from Mumbai, Riya's hopes for continued contact with the charming person she had met were dashed. As days turned into weeks and then into months, Riya was confused. He disappeared without a trace, leaving Riya feeling disappointed. Riya couldn't help but dwell on the memories of the conversations, laughter, and genuine connection she had shared with the charming person. Despite their brief encounter, those few hours had left a lasting impression on her. It was difficult for her to accept that someone could seemingly forget those moments so easily. She replayed their conversations in her mind, reliving the moments of laughter and connection they had shared. It felt real to her, and she couldn't understand how someone could not keep a touch and act as if it never happened. The authenticity of their interaction made it challenging for Riya to come to terms with the sudden disappearance and apparent lack of interest. Riya questioned herself, wondering if she had misread the situation or if there was something she had done wrong. She couldn't fathom how someone could create such a genuine connection, only to vanish without a trace. It left her feeling a mix of confusion, disappointment, and even a tinge of sadness. She contemplated reaching out to Vidya as he was their mutual friend, but hesitated, fearing it might come across as unnecessary desperation. Besides, she was unsure if the guy was even interested in her.

However, as time passed, Riya began to realize that dwelling on the situation wouldn't change the outcome. While the memory of their encounter lingered, Riya gradually accepted that sometimes people enter our lives for a brief period and then fade away. She chose to focus on her own growth, embracing the lessons she had learned from the experience. She understood that she couldn't control someone else's actions or feelings, but she had the power to choose how she responded and moved forward. As time went on and the charming person remained absent from Riya's life, she gradually moved on from her feelings for him.

During the scorching summers in Delhi, the intense heat can be quite challenging to bear, and it's crucial to take caution and care to protect oneself from sunstroke and heat-related illnesses. The soaring temperatures often necessitate certain lifestyle adjustments to ensure well-being. Due to the extreme heat, it's common for people in Delhi to avoid going outdoors during the hottest part of the day, usually between 12 PM and 3 PM. This period is when the sun's rays are the strongest and can be particularly harmful. Instead, individuals tend to plan their activities either in the early morning or late afternoon when the temperatures are relatively cooler.

Staying hydrated is of utmost importance during the summer months. People in Delhi ensure they drink an ample amount of water and other hydrating beverages throughout the day to prevent dehydration. They carry water bottles with them and make it a habit to replenish their fluid intake frequently. Popular summer beverages like lemonade, Panna water, and buttermilk are also consumed to stay refreshed and hydrated. To cope with the heat, individuals in Delhi choose clothing that allows for maximum comfort and ventilation. Lightweight and loose-fitting fabrics, such as cotton, are preferred to help the body stay cool. Wearing light-coloured clothes that reflect sunlight is also common practice as they absorb less heat. Additionally, protecting oneself from direct sunlight by wearing hats, covering head with a cotton cloth, sunglasses, and applying sunscreen is essential when venturing outdoors.

Riya, a captivating embodiment of grace and elegance, carries herself with the effortless charm of a true fashion connoisseur. Her slender frame and poised demeanour are a reflection of her upbringing in a family deeply immersed in the world of fashion. As her wavy, dark brown hair cascades down her back, it serves as the perfect complement to her almond-shaped eyes and warm smile, radiating a magnetic allure. Impeccable fashion sense is second nature to Riya, effortlessly blending traditional and modern styles with an artistic finesse. Her outfits are carefully chosen to showcase her individuality while paying homage to her family's legacy in the garment industry. Driven by an insatiable thirst for knowledge and a burning passion for law and business, Riya is a force to be reckoned with. A diligent and ambitious individual, she possesses a sharp intellect that lends itself well to the complexities of legal matters. Her natural aptitude for problem-solving makes her a formidable presence in any professional setting, always seeking new challenges to test her limits and expand her horizons.

Having been raised in a family deeply rooted in the business world, Riya's upbringing has bestowed upon her a strong work ethic and an determination. Her family's successful business in garment, renowned for its intricately designed langaas for weddings and ceremonies, has instilled in her a profound understanding of entrepreneurship from an early age. Her keen eye for market trends and her ability to identify opportunities for growth set her apart as a visionary. Beyond her intellectual pursuits, Riya possesses a multitude of diverse hobbies and interests. A voracious reader, she delves into legal thrillers and business biographies, continually expanding her knowledge and gaining insights into the global market landscape. Engaging in spirited discussions with her family, she navigates the intricacies of the garment industry, fuelled by her passion for its intricacies.

Riya's aspirations transcend the boundaries of her individual pursuits. With her legal acumen and business expertise, she envisions herself making a significant contribution to the growth and success of her family's business. She dreams of working in close collaboration with her father and brother to explore untapped markets and expand their garment exports to new horizons. However, Riya's ambitions do not end there. Her grand vision includes establishing a prestigious legal consultancy firm exclusively catered to the fashion industry. Through this endeavour, she aims to provide indispensable legal guidance and support to businesses in the fashion world, ensuring their operations thrive in a dynamic and ever-evolving landscape. Riya's burning desire to pursue specialized studies in international trade law abroad and expand her family's garment exports to untapped markets stirred a whirlwind of emotions within her family. The prospect of Riya venturing into uncharted territories and bringing global exposure to their business evoked both excitement and apprehension. While they couldn't help but feel a twinge of concern about her venturing abroad for her education, they also couldn't deny the fire in her eyes and the determination in her voice. Riya's ambitions resonated deeply with their shared vision of global success, but the thought of their beloved daughter being far away tugged at their hearts.

As the news of Riya's decision to study abroad settled within the family, debates and discussions filled the family gatherings as they weighed the pros and cons of

Riya's international pursuit. There were sleepless nights and moments of apprehension, but beneath it all, there was an belief in Riya's potential. Her parents exchanged worried glances, unsure about the implications and challenges of Riya being in an unfamiliar place. Her mother, with a hint of hesitation in her voice, asked, "Riya, are you sure about going abroad for your education? It's such a big step, and we'll miss you dearly."

Riya's father, mustering a smile, chimed in, "She's always been ambitious, my dear. We must trust her instincts and support her dreams." Uncles and aunts shared their own concerns, expressing their fears of Riya being so far from home. But Riya, with firm determination, looked at them and said, "I understand your worries, and I truly appreciate your love and concern. But I believe this opportunity will not only benefit me but also our family's business. I want to bring back knowledge and experiences that will help us reach new heights."

As the discussions unfolded, Riya took the initiative to address their concerns, reassuring them of her careful planning and commitment to her education and the family's business. Her older brother, a source of constant support, put a reassuring hand on her shoulder. "You've always been the brightest among us, Riya. We're proud of you and believe in your abilities." Her father, her rock and mentor, added, "Promise me you'll take care of yourself, Riya. Study hard, but also remember to enjoy life."

Riya's mother, her voice filled with a mix of pride and worry, added, "Promise me you'll take care of yourself, Riya. Riya embraced her mother tightly, assuring her, "I promise, Mom. I'll make the most of this opportunity while cherishing our family values and staying connected with all of you."

Slowly, reservations gave way to acceptance, and

acceptance blossomed into enthusiastic support. Riya's family understood that shielding her from the world would only limit her growth and potential. They realized that by allowing her to spread her wings and soar beyond the familiar, she would acquire insights, experiences, and skills that would propel their business to unprecedented heights. With each passing day, their pride swelled, mingling with a bittersweet anticipation. They were sending off their jewel, their brightest star, into the vast expanse of the unknown. But they did so with faith, knowing that Riya possessed the strength, resilience, and tenacity to conquer any challenge that came her way. When the news of her admission to the prestigious international university (Columbia University, New York state) finally arrived, their home erupted in joyous celebration. Tears of pride and excitement flowed freely, mingling with laughter and hugs. she shared the news with all her friends and provided them with her contact details to stay in touch.

The days that followed were a flurry of preparations, as Riya meticulously planned her journey, armed with determination and an insatiable thirst for knowledge. Her family rallied around her, ensuring every detail was taken care of, from visas to accommodations. They were her backbone, her rock, and their firm support fortified her spirit. As the day of departure, emotions ran high. Riya's parents watched her packing her bags, their emotions palpable. Her father, with a lump in his throat, said, "You're our shining star, Riya. Reach for the stars and make your dreams come true." With tears glistening in her eyes, her mother added, "Remember, you carry our love and support wherever you go. We'll be waiting for you to return and share your incredible journey with us." Riya embraced her parents tightly, assuring them, "I promise, I shall make you proud" with tearful farewells and heartfelt words of encouragement, Riya embarked on her journey, knowing that she carried the hopes and dreams of her family within her. As the wheels of the aircraft lifted off the ground, Riya glanced out the window, her heart filled with a mix of emotions. She couldn't help but feel a profound gratitude for her family, whose belief in her had set her on this incredible path.

THREE
Threads of Collaboration

As the monsoon rain poured outside, Riya sat in her cozy living room in New York, scrolling through her social media feed. The sound of raindrops hitting the windowpane created a soothing backdrop to her thoughts. Lost in the rhythm of the rainfall, she absentmindedly checked her notifications and noticed a friend request from someone unfamiliar.

Curiosity piqued, Riya clicked on the profile and scanned through the photos and posts. The person seemed to have mutual friends, which made her wonder how they were connected. Intrigued, she accepted the friend request, unknowingly stepping into a world that would turn her life upside down. Days turned into weeks, and as the rain continued to pour, Riya's online interactions with this mysterious person named Raj became more frequent. He began commenting on her posts, adding witty remarks and insightful observations. His words resonated with her, and she found herself eagerly awaiting his next comment, his next virtual presence.

Unbeknownst to Riya, Raj was the charming personality she had met in Mumbai, masquerading behind a fake profile. As he observed her life through the virtual window, he discovered layers of her personality that had captivated him during their brief encounter. Her kindness, intelligence, and depth of character shone through her posts, drawing him in like a moth to a flame. During Riya's time abroad, their virtual connection continued to flourish. They conversed regularly, sharing their thoughts, experiences, and even their dreams for the future. The geographical distance between them seemed inconsequential as their bond grew stronger with each passing day. As time passed, their interactions on social media gradually increased, and they found comfort and joy in each other's virtual company. Being far away from home and friends, Riya cherished the moments spent talking to him. He kept her busy and engaged with interesting conversations, jokes, and his delightful sense of humor. While Riya made friends in her new environment, there was something uniquely captivating and endearing about this particular connection.

The conversations they had were filled with laughter, deep discussions, and moments of vulnerability. They supported each other through the ups and downs of life, offering words of encouragement and understanding. Despite the physical distance, they found solace in their virtual companionship. As Riya explored new cultures and experiences in a foreign land, she often found herself sharing her adventures and challenges and learnings with him. She cherished the way he listened attentively, offering genuine interest and support from afar. Their connection became an anchor in her life, a source of comfort and familiarity in a world of newness.

Meanwhile, he eagerly awaited her updates, living vicariously through her stories and experiences. He took joy in the fact that they were able to maintain such a strong connection despite the miles between them. Their conversations became a highlight of his day, an opportunity to escape the monotony of everyday life and be transported into Riya's world. During this time, their feelings for each other deepened. What began as a casual interaction had blossomed into something special. They shared a unique understanding and emotional intimacy that transcended physical proximity.

As Riya's time abroad drew to a close, they both realized that they wanted to explore their connection further. They yearned to meet in person, to bridge the gap between their virtual interactions and real-life encounters. The anticipation of finally being able to see each other face-to-face filled them with excitement and nervousness. With each passing day, their affection and longing grew stronger. They had formed a bond that surpassed the limitations of distance and time zones. The prospect of finally meeting and exploring the depths of their connection filled them both with anticipation and a sense of adventure.

During the period, smart phones and video calling were not as advanced or readily available as they are today. As a result, people primarily relied on more traditional methods of communication to stay in touch with friends and family abroad. Emails became an essential means of communication during this time and Facebook as a means to connect with friends and family members, sharing life events, photos, and personal thoughts through posts and comments.

Back home, Riya's family embraced a period of exciting growth and expansion in their thriving family business. Brother and father were actively involved in expanding their enterprise both internationally and nationally. Their vision for growth and their commitment to innovation kept them on the lookout for new opportunities. During this time, an exciting development took place in Delhi - the government organized a conference called "New Delhi with New Innovations" and invited business enterprises and leaders from across India to participate.

This conference aimed to bring together industry experts,

entrepreneurs, and innovators to discuss the future prospects of business in Delhi. It provided a platform for networking, knowledge sharing, and the announcement of new initiatives and opportunities in the city. Riya's brother, Parminder being proactive and eager to explore fresh avenues for their business, saw this conference as a perfect opportunity to expand their horizons and discover new possibilities. The conference brought together a diverse range of business leaders, government officials, and industry experts. It featured panel discussions, keynote speeches, and interactive sessions that explored various sectors and highlighted the potential for innovation and growth in Delhi. Prominent figures from the business community shared their success stories, best practices, and insights, inspiring others to embrace new ideas and contribute to the development of the city.

For Malhotra's family, this conference served as a platform to showcase their business achievements and connect with potential partners, investors, and clients. They actively engaged in networking activities, seeking collaborations and exploring avenues for expansion. It was an opportunity to share their expertise and learn from other industry leaders, gaining valuable insights into market trends, emerging technologies, and government policies that could impact their business. The conference also presented an opportunity to contribute to the growth and development of Delhi's business landscape. Malhotra's, both father and son actively participated in discussions and brainstorming sessions, sharing their perspectives and ideas on how to foster innovation, attract investments, and create a favourable business environment in the city. They recognized the importance of collaboration between the government and the private sector to drive economic growth and promote entrepreneurship.

The "New Delhi with New Innovations" conference left

a lasting impact on Malhotra's and their business. It expanded their network, opened doors to potential partnerships and collaborations, and provided them with valuable insights into the future direction of the business landscape in Delhi. During the three-day conference, Riya's brother Parminder had the opportunity to meet Rohan, and their interaction sparked a cordial and constructive business discussion. As they exchanged ideas and explored potential collaborations, it became evident that they shared a common vision for business expansion in Delhi. Rohan, impressed by Parminder's local knowledge, financial stability, intelligence, and his family's long-standing business background, saw him as a perfect match for the new business opportunity he had in mind. Recognizing Parminder's potential and the value he could bring to the venture, Rohan proposed joining forces as business partners to explore the Delhi market together and exploring global market in near future.

Excited by the proposition and intrigued by the potential of the new business opportunity, Parminder agreed to carefully evaluate Rohan's business plan. Recognizing the importance of thorough analysis and due diligence, he expressed his willingness to review the proposal in detail and meet again to discuss the specifics. In the days following the conference, Parminder dedicated his time and resources to carefully examining Rohan's business plan. He analysed the market potential, evaluated the financial projections, and assessed the feasibility and alignment with their family business goals. As he dove deeper into the details, Parminder became increasingly optimistic about the prospects of partnering with Rohan. After thorough consideration and discussion with his family, Parminder decided to meet Rohan again to further explore the potential collaboration. He appreciated the professionalism and integrity Rohan had displayed during their initial conversation and believed that their partnership had the potential to create a strong business presence in Delhi.

The subsequent meeting between Parminder and Rohan delved into the finer aspects of the business plan, addressing concerns, and solidifying their shared vision. They discussed the allocation of responsibilities, financial arrangements, and long-term growth strategies. With each interaction, their trust and confidence in each other's abilities grew, strengthening their resolve to embark on this new business venture together. Finally, after extensive negotiations and deliberations, Parminder and Rohan agreed to form a partnership, combining their expertise, resources, and networks. The alliance promised to leverage their respective strengths and create a formidable presence in the Delhi market.

This exciting collaboration between Parminder and Rohan opened doors to new opportunities for their family business, marking a significant milestone in their journey of expansion. Recognizing the potential of the international market, they decided to venture into the realm of garments and accessories, aiming to represent the rich cultural heritage of India in various countries across the globe. Their tie-up involved forging strategic alliances with renowned international retailers and distributors, allowing them to showcase their exquisite range of garments and accessories to a global audience. They carefully curated a collection that celebrated the vibrant colours, intricate designs, and impeccable craftsmanship that India was known for.

With Rohan's expertise in international trade and market trends, they identified key target markets and tailored their offerings to cater to the preferences and tastes of consumers in those regions. They embarked on a journey of cultural exchange, bridging the gap between different countries and fostering a deeper appreciation for Indian textiles and craftsmanship.

Their collaboration went beyond just business transactions. It was driven by a shared vision of promoting India's rich cultural heritage and empowering local artisans and craftsmen. They worked closely with grassroots organizations and cooperatives, ensuring fair trade practices and sustainable sourcing of materials. The tie-up also involved participating in renowned international trade fairs and exhibitions, where they showcased their exclusive collection and connected with potential buyers and distributors. Through these platforms, they aimed to position their brand as a symbol of quality, authenticity, and style, representing India's unique identity on the global stage. They started traveling together and exploring new dimension and perspectives for business. In the process they became good friends.

The partnership brought together the strengths of both Parminder's family business and Rohan's new venture, creating a powerful synergy that allowed them to overcome challenges and leverage opportunities in the competitive international market. Their combined expertise, resources, and networks enabled them to establish a strong presence in various countries, expanding their customer base and generating increased demand for their products. By representing India in various countries, they not only aimed to boost exports and contribute to the country's economy but also to promote cross-cultural understanding and appreciation. Within a short period they became ambassadors of Indian craftsmanship, showcasing the beauty and elegance of traditional garments and accessories to the world.

Rohan exudes confidence and charisma, effortlessly drawing attention with his striking physical appearance. His well-groomed and polished look reflects his attention to detail and professionalism, while his tall and athletic build adds to his commanding presence. Sophistication and refinement define his sense of style, often seen in tailored suits that convey authority and elegance. Rohan's facial features are sharp and defined, complemented by a well-maintained beard that adds a touch of maturity and sophistication. His focused gaze radiates determination and ambition.

Residing in Mumbai, Rohan embodies ambition and determination, fuelled by his dream of becoming a millionaire. He relentlessly pursues success and refuses to settle for mediocrity. As a successful entrepreneur running multiple thriving ventures, Rohan's business acumen and ability to identify lucrative opportunities shine through. Calculated risks hold no fear for him, understanding they lead to great rewards. His drive motivates constant innovation and growth.

While reserved at first, Rohan's ability to impress others comes alive when engaged in conversation. His wit and charm captivate those around him. Living independently in Mumbai, Rohan has embraced responsibilities, cultivating discipline and adaptability. Despite the physical distance from his family in Nagpur, he holds them close to his heart, cherishing the support and happiness they bring. Rohan 's living arrangement also allows him to fully immerse himself in his work, dedicating his time and energy to his business ventures. Born and raised in Mumbai, the vibrant city nurtures Rohan's entrepreneurial spirit. It offers ample networking opportunities and fuels his ambition. Yet, he remains grounded and compassionate, emphasizing personal growth and continuous education and looking more opportunities.

FOUR
Unravelling Conflicts

As Riya sat in the dimly lit cabin of the plane, her mind raced with anticipation and concern. The flight back to her homeland was filled with a mix of excitement and unease, unsure of what awaited her upon her arrival. The distant hum of the airplane engines seemed to echo her own restless thoughts. Finally, the wheels touched down, and Riya's heart raced with a sense of urgency. She hastily gathered her belongings and made her way through the bustling airport. Her eyes searched the crowd for a familiar face, until she finally spotted her father, standing tall amidst the sea of strangers.

Their eyes met, and without exchanging any words, a world of emotions passed between them. Riya could see the worry etched on her father's face, lines that hadn't been there before. She could sense the weight of unspoken turmoil hanging in the air. As they embraced, a mix of relief and apprehension washed over Riya. She knew her father wouldn't have called her back unless it was something significant, something that demanded her immediate attention. Their journey from the airport to their home was shrouded in silence, with both of them lost in their own thoughts. As they entered the familiar surroundings of their home, the air seemed heavy with unspoken words. Riya's eyes darted around, taking in the subtle changes in the decor and the stillness that hung in the atmosphere. She longed for answers, for her brother to reveal the reason behind his urgent call.

After a year and a half of being away from her family, Riya's heart was filled with joy and with anticipation as why suddenly she was been called back. But she was happy to unite with her loved ones and sharing all what she is been doing all this years. Over a sumptuous dinner, Riya recounted her experiences in New York, sharing tales of bustling courtrooms, intense negotiations, and the intricacies of international trade law. Her family listened with rapt attention, marvelling at her growth and the opportunities she had seized. Her cousin Simran, her eyes wide with admiration, asked, "Did you ever feel overwhelmed, did you miss us?"

Riya smiled, her voice tinged with nostalgia, "Of course, I had my moments of homesickness, but the excitement of the work and the chance to make a difference kept me going. And I could always feel your love and support, even from across the miles." Her father, beaming with pride, added, "We knew you would shine, Riya. You've always had that spark within you."

As the evening progressed, Riya couldn't help but notice the genuine curiosity in her family's eyes. They wanted to know more about her work, her accomplishments, and the opportunities that lay ahead. The thought of exploring new avenues and making even greater contributions filled her with a renewed sense of purpose. Mother asked " how was your work?" "I've been fortunate enough to work on some remarkable cases and projects," Riya shared, her voice filled with excitement. "And now, I have the chance to take on even more responsibility. The firm sees potential in me and has offered me an opportunity to work on a high-profile international trade agreement. It's a chance to showcase my skills on a global stage." Her mother's eyes sparkled with a mixture of pride and concern.

Riya's heart swelled with gratitude, but her eyes was searching for her brother and few things are still unanswered. Finally, the moment arrived when Riya's brother, Parminder, entered the room. His face, once filled with cheerfulness and enthusiasm, now carried a burdened expression. Riya could see the weight of responsibility resting on his shoulders, and it only deepened her curiosity. Gathering around the family, they sat in a circle, the room enveloped in a solemn hush. Parminder took a deep breath, his voice quivering with a mix of anxiety and frustration. The weight of the crisis bore heavily on his shoulders as he mustered the courage to share the fearsome reality that had befallen their family business.

"I never imagined we would face such daunting challenges," Parminder began, his voice filled with a mixture of concern and disbelief. "In recent months, we've encountered unexpected hurdles that have shaken the very foundation of everything we've worked so hard to build", "Our accounts have been abruptly frozen," Parminder continued, his words laced with a sense of helplessness. "International buyers, who trusted us with their orders, are now demanding both money and products back. But, to our horror, we discovered that our account was emptied overnight, leaving us bewildered and questioning where our hard-earned money disappeared to."

The depth of the crisis became even more apparent as Parminder continued, his voice trembling with a hint of frustration. "Not only have we lost our funds, but our credit lines have been completely exhausted. It feels like we're trapped in a suffocating financial abyss."

The situation took a sinister turn as Parminder revealed, "Multiple unauthorized international transactions have been observed from our account. It's clear that someone purposely and intentionally tried to hack into our financial system, leaving us vulnerable and exposed."

Parminder's worry and desperation became palpable as he expressed, "I've been grappling with this on my own, hoping I could handle it, but now, it's spiralling out of control. The bank is demanding details, and even the IT company has raised alarms about the breach. I'm deeply concerned about the implications for our business and the uncertainty that lies ahead." As Parminder shared these heart-wrenching details, his voice carried a plea for understanding and support. "I couldn't bear the burden alone any longer. We need help, expertise, and guidance to navigate this crisis and regain control over our financial affairs. The weight of our employees' livelihoods and the future of our business rests heavily on my shoulders, and I'm determined to find a way forward."

The weight of Parminder's revelation hung heavily in the air, leaving the entire family in a state of shock and disbelief. Their faces reflected a mix of confusion, concern, and deep-rooted worry as they tried to comprehend the magnitude of the crisis that had befallen their cherished family business. They exchanged glances, their eyes filled with a mix of fear and disbelief. The once bustling household now stood in silence, as if time had momentarily frozen. It was as if the ground beneath them had shifted, leaving them unsteady and uncertain about the future. Unspoken questions lingered in the room. How could this have happened? Who could have orchestrated such a malicious act against their family? The gravity of the situation began to sink in, and a sense of urgency swept through their hearts, urging them to find answers and solutions to salvage what remained of their shattered financial stability.

Riya's heart sank as she absorbed the details of her

family's business struggles. She could sense the weight of concern in the room, and a deep sense of responsibility surged within her. There was an underlying sense that something wasn't quite right, a feeling that tugged at her intuition. She knew she needed the full picture before making any judgments or decisions. Her mind raced with a mix of concern and determination. She realized that her brother had called her back not only for support but also for her expertise in international trade law, to help navigate the storm that had engulfed their family's legacy. As Parminder finished recounting the story. She turned to her brother Parminder, their eyes locking in a moment of shared understanding.

Riya: (gently) Parminder, I can't begin to comprehend the magnitude of what we're facing. How did it come to this? Our accounts frozen, international buyers demanding payment, and unauthorized transactions draining our resources... It's unfathomable.

Parminder: (frustrated) Riya, it feels like a nightmare. We trusted the wrong people, and now our family's legacy is hanging by a thread. I don't know where to turn or how to make things right.

Riya took a deep breath, her mind racing with thoughts of strategy and solutions. She turned to their father, who had been silently observing the conversation, his face etched with worry.

Riya: (firmly) Dad, we can't let despair consume us. We need to gather our strength and face this head-on. We have each other, and together, we can overcome this crisis. It's time to fight back and reclaim what's rightfully ours.

Father: (nodding, determination in his voice) You're right, Riya. Our family has weathered storms before, and we've always emerged stronger. We must unite, pool our expertise, and find a way to rectify this situation.

As they immersed themselves in discussions late into the

night, Riya felt a sense of belonging and purpose. The journey that brought her back home had unfolded in unexpected ways, but she was ready to face the challenges head-on, armed with her knowledge, determination, and the unshakeable support of her family. Little did she know that this chapter in her life would test her in ways she had never imagined. Recognizing the complexity of the issues at hand, she realized the importance of seeking expert guidance. Riya sat down with her father to discuss their urgent need for a legal team. She knew time was of the essence, and finding someone specialized in their specific matter was crucial.

Riya leaned forward, a determined look in her eyes, and said, "Father, we need to act swiftly and find the right lawyer for our situation. Do we know anyone who specializes in this area? It would be a great help if we have someone with expertise in international trade law."

Her father nodded, understanding the urgency. "You're right, Riya. We can't afford to delay. Let's make some calls and see if we can find someone suitable." He reached for his phone and began dialling, while Riya started researching and calling too. The family worked tirelessly, making phone calls and reaching out to their network.

Next day morning, they finally received a positive lead. Riya's father looked up from his phone, a glimmer of relief in his eyes. "I've managed to secure an appointment with a highly recommended lawyer and consultant. They come highly recommended and have extensive experience in handling complex business disputes and international trade matters."

Riya's face lit up with hope. "That's great news, Father! It seems like a step in the right direction. We should meet them as soon as possible and discuss our situation in detail." Her father nodded in agreement. "Yes, we should.

Riya. It's important that we choose the best legal support for our family's business." And I've already taken appointment for us."

While they were engrossed in their discussion, a sudden, loud knock echoed through the room, jolting everyone from their thoughts. The atmosphere instantly turned tense as Parminder hurriedly made his way to the door. He cautiously opened it and was handed an envelope by an unfamiliar figure. The envelope bore official markings, instantly grabbing everyone's attention. Parminder's hands trembled as he tore open the envelope, revealing its contents. As he began reading the letter, his face turned pale, and a mix of shock and disbelief swept across his features. The room fell into an eerie silence, broken only by the sound of heavy breathing and racing hearts. The letter contained a legal notice accompanied by an arrest warrant, setting off a tidal wave of panic and confusion that washed over the entire family.

Riya's eyes widened with disbelief as she scanned the contents of the letter. "Arrest warrant? But how? This can't be happening!" she exclaimed, her voice filled with a mixture of fear and anxiety. Her father's voice quivered as he struggled to find the right words. "We need to stay calm and gather all the information. Parminder, did the letter mention any specifics?"

Parminder nodded, his voice trembling as he relayed the shocking details. "It's related to a business transaction gone wrong, Father. They are accusing us of fraud and illegal practices. We need to act quickly and find a way to resolve this." The room filled with a chorus of worried voices as the family tried to make sense of the situation. The air was thick with tension and uncertainty, their minds racing to comprehend the gravity of the accusations and the potential consequences.

Riya's mother, her voice laced with concern, spoke up. "We must reach out to the lawyer immediately. We need their guidance and expertise now more than ever." Riya, nodded in agreement. "You're right, Mother. This situation requires immediate action and legal counsel. We can't afford to waste any time."

The gravity of the situation began to sink in as they realized the potential consequences they were facing. Questions swirled in their minds, demanding answers they were not yet prepared to confront. Riya's father, usually a pillar of strength, appeared visibly shaken. His face lined with worry, he struggled to find the words to explain the situation to his family. The weight of their uncertain future hung heavily in the air, casting a shadow over their once-thriving business and their collective dreams.

The sudden arrival of the legal notice sent shockwaves through their lives, shaking the very foundation of their family and business. It was a stark reminder of the challenges and risks inherent in the world of commerce, and the consequences that could arise from unforeseen circumstances. As they absorbed the news, their minds raced with questions and concerns. What had led to this situation? Who was behind these allegations? And most importantly, how would they defend themselves and protect their family's reputation?

FIVE

Shadows of Uncertainty

Riya and her father arrived at the legal office, located in the heart of the bustling city centre. The tall office building exuded confidence amidst the bustling city street. The modern reception area welcomed Riya and her father with its polished marble floors and prestigious awards on display. Friendly staff directed them to the designated meeting room, where passionate lawyers worked diligently on their cases in glass-walled offices. As they entered the meeting room, Riya and her father were greeted by their legal team. The tastefully furnished room with law books and legal references created a professional and inviting atmosphere. The large conference table served as the focal point, surrounded by windows offering cityscape views and ample natural light. It was ideal for productive discussions and planning.

As the legal team gathered, a sense of seriousness and purpose filled the air. Just as tension peaked, the door swung open, revealing a figure of authority. With a dashing personality and confident demeanor, they immediately captivated everyone's attention. Tall and well-groomed, Siddharth Malhotra exuded power and charisma. As one of the esteemed partners of the legal firm, his name carried a reputation of expertise in the field of law, commanding respect and attention. With a warm yet confident smile, he extended his hand to Riya and her father, welcoming her into the discussion. As

Riya heard the name "Malhotra," her eyes rolled, but she kept her thoughts to herself, extending a handshake to Siddharth. What a coincidence and funny at the same time, she thought, as there seemed to be so many Malhotras in Delhi. His firm handshake conveyed both professionalism and a genuine desire to help.

As the discussion progressed, Siddharth Malhotra's strategic thinking and problem-solving skills shone through. He guided the legal team with precision, encouraging collaborative brainstorming and fostering an environment of innovation and creativity. He outlined the next steps in the legal proceedings, providing a clear roadmap for the path ahead. As the meeting progressed, Siddharth Malhotra posed a crucial question that demanded attention. His tone conveyed a mix of curiosity, determination, and a touch of concern. "Who is this individual? Do we have any prior business relationship or family connects with this guy or company? Siddharth asked, emphasizing the importance of understanding the person responsible for orchestrating such a meticulously planned situation. Riya's father responded with a tense and somewhat frustrated tone, expressing how he and his son Parminder had met the partner for the first time during the Delhi conference that had taken place a couple of years ago. He explained that they had seen it as a great business opportunity and had conducted their due diligence before accepting the partner's proposal. All went well for few years and then one fine day Partner introduce us this person as a potential buyer for international business and we went ahead with him. However, he lamented the fact that they couldn't have foreseen the turn of events and the subsequent legal troubles that followed.

He acknowledged the unpredictable nature of business partnerships and how sometimes things could go awry despite careful consideration and research. In this particular case, the partner had seemingly acted in a deceptive and malicious manner, putting the family and their business in a precarious situation and reason for this new association is not clear. Siddharth probed further, seeking to understand why it had taken Riya and her family so long to seek legal assistance. "Why did it take you so long to approach a legal team in Delhi?" Siddharth asked, his tone both inquisitive and empathetic. He recognized that there might be underlying reasons or hesitations that had hindered their prompt action. Riya's father shared their concerns and explained that they had initially tried to handle the situation themselves, hoping it would resolve on its own.

However, as the threats escalated and the legal implications became apparent, they realized the need for professional guidance and representation. Siddharth listened attentively, understanding the complexity of their emotions and the challenges they faced. Siddharth Malhotra highlighted an important aspect of the case: it had been registered in the Mumbai court. He explained that while he would make efforts to bring the case to the Delhi court for their convenience, he couldn't make any promises due to the involvement of the other partner. Siddharth clarified that the partner who had filed the case against Riya's brother had his corporate office in Mumbai and resided there as well. This meant that the legal proceedings would likely take place in Mumbai, given the jurisdiction and convenience of the parties involved.

However, Siddharth assured Riya and her family that he would explore all possible legal avenues to facilitate the transfer of the case to a Delhi court. He understood the challenges they would face if the proceedings were conducted in Mumbai, and he empathized with their desire to have the case heard closer to their home. With time running out, the team made every effort to ensure that all the required paperwork was accurately completed and filed before the deadline. The weight of the impending legal battle hung in the air, but the legal team remained resolute in their commitment to defending Riya's family and seeking justice against those who had wronged them. The filing time approached its final moments, and the legal team double-checked their work, making sure that everything was in order. Siddharth Malhotra, as the leader of the team, with a tone of urgency, addressed Riya's father, "Mr. Balminder, time is of the essence. If we delay any further, the consequences could become even more serious. We must respond to the notice immediately, and for that, I suggest you go ahead and appoint our legal team, Malhotra and Sons, as your lawyers."

After carefully considering Siddharth's advice and evaluating the expertise of Malhotra and Sons, Balminder nodded in agreement. He reached for the pen and signed the papers, solidifying the appointment of the legal team. As he set the pen down, he looked at Siddharth and said, "I trust your judgment, Siddharth. This firm seems to be the right choice for my son and our family." Siddharth, visibly pleased with the decision, replied, "You've made the right decision, I have full confidence that Malhotra and Sons will handle the legal matters with utmost professionalism and expertise."

Riya, her voice filled with concern, added, "Father, we need to act swiftly and decisively. The legal team will guide us through this process and help protect our interests." Siddharth, nodded with agreement and said, "we will initiate the necessary steps to address the notice and defend our case immediately."

Siddharth, concerned about Parminder's absence, turned to Riya and inquired, "Riya, where is Parminder? Why isn't he here in my office discussing the details with us? We need to gather all the necessary information and understand his perspective. Please arrange a meeting with him as soon as possible.".

Riya nodded, understanding the importance of including Parminder in the discussions. She replied, "I agree, Siddharth but Parminder is currently not in a condition to travel and Parminder's insights are crucial for us to gain a comprehensive understanding of the situation. I will reach out to him will set up an appointment for us to meet tomorrow at your office." Siddharth nodded, acknowledging Riya's explanation. "Understood, Riya. Let's schedule the appointment for tomorrow, and we can proceed with our discussions then." With their conversation concluded, Riya gathered her belongings and left the office, Leaving the office, Riya and her father carried a mixture of hope and uncertainty. They knew that the road ahead would be arduous.

In the midst of the crisis and the pressing legal matters, Riya's mind was consumed with the urgent issues at hand. The weight of the situation overshadowed her thoughts about Raj and her friends. Days turned into weeks, and her hectic schedule left little room for personal matters. While Riya was dealing with the legal proceedings and supporting her family, the thought of reaching out to Raj and her friends slipped through the cracks. It wasn't intentional; rather, it was a result of the overwhelming circumstances she found herself in.

As time went on, the days blended together, and Riya's focus remained on the impending legal battle and finding a way to protect her family's interests. The emotional and mental toll of the situation made it difficult for her to remember the connections she had made during her time abroad and the relationships she had built. Amidst the chaos and stress, Riya's mind was consumed by legal consultations, discussions with her family, and gathering evidence for their defence. She barely had time to catch her breath, let alone think about her personal relationships.

Riya's heart longed for the comfort of her friends and the familiarity of their companionship. With her upcoming trip to Mumbai on the horizon, she saw it as an opportunity to reconnect with Raj and her circle of friends who resided in the city. She reached out to them, hoping to find solace and support in their presence during this challenging time. As she composed her messages, Riya's mind wandered to the memories she had shared with Raj and her friends. They had been there for each other through thick and thin, supporting one another during both joyous and difficult times. The thought of rekindling those connections brought a glimmer of hope to her troubled heart.

She eagerly awaited their responses, hoping for warm words and an enthusiastic embrace of her desire to reconnect. She knew that Raj, in particular, had played a significant role in her life, even though she was yet unaware of his true identity behind the fake profile. Their virtual interactions had sparked something within her, and she yearned to explore the possibility of a deeper connection in person. She hoped that their presence would provide a much-needed respite from the weight of the legal battles and uncertainties that engulfed her family. She needed her friends by her side. Little did she know that her reunion with Raj and her friends would bring forth unexpected revelations and confrontations, leading to a turning point in her journey.

Siddharth Malhotra, a prominent and esteemed figure in the legal field, has built a remarkable reputation for himself over the years. Born and raised in Delhi, he pursued his higher education at Delhi University, where he studied law. With a deep passion for justice and a sharp legal mind, Siddharth joined a prestigious legal firm eight years ago, embarking on a successful career that has seen him soar to great heights. Siddharth comes from a family with a rich legal legacy. His grandfather laid the foundation of Malhotra and Sons, a renowned legal firm that has been serving clients for over 80 years. Siddharth takes great pride in carrying on this family legacy, upholding the values of integrity, professionalism, and dedication that have become synonymous with the firm.

On a personal level, Siddharth has faced his fair share of challenges. He experienced a painful divorce from his wife, who had betrayed him by having an affair with his close friend. This betrayal led to the dissolution of their marriage, and his ex-wife now resides in Dubai. Despite the personal turmoil he endured, Siddharth found solace and support in the strong love of his parents, with whom he shares a close bond. They provide him with a strong support system, helping him navigate both personal and professional aspects of his life. Known for his exceptional legal acumen, Siddharth has never lost a case throughout his illustrious career. His impressive track record has earned him the trust and respect of clients and colleagues alike. His meticulous approach to his work, combined with his deep understanding of the law, has made him a force to be reckoned with in the legal community. Beyond his legal expertise, Siddharth carries himself with an air of sophistication and elegance. His impeccable professionalism and charismatic demeanour leave a lasting impression on those he encounters. He is known for his commitment to justice, fighting tirelessly to protect the rights of his clients and ensuring a fair and equitable legal system.

As Siddharth joins forces with Riya and her family, his invaluable expertise and determination become pivotal in their pursuit of justice. His presence instils a sense of confidence and reassurance, knowing that they are in the hands of a legal powerhouse who will leave no stone unturned in their battle for truth and justice.

Riya's father, Balminder, Parminder and Siddharth understood the urgency of the situation and the need to gather the necessary evidence to prove Parminder's innocence. With the deadline looming, they all made their way to Mumbai to file for an extension and request additional time to collect the required documents. Upon reaching the legal firm's Mumbai office, they were greeted by a bustling atmosphere filled with lawyers and clients engaged in various legal matters. The office was located in a prime area of the city, reflecting the firm's prominence and reputation. The interior of the office exuded professionalism and efficiency, with sleek furnishings, modern technology, and well-organized workspaces.

Siddharth Malhotra, leading the way with confidence, guided Riya's father, Parminder and the legal team through the corridors of the office, a well-appointed conference room, the legal team gathered around a large table, They were prepared to present a compelling case for an extension, and further proceedings in Delhi court, emphasizing the critical nature of the situation and the need for more time to secure the evidence that would clear Parminder's name. His keen eyes scanned through the documents and evidence, assessing their strength and potential impact on the case. Siddharth listened attentively to the Mumbai legal team's arguments too, interjecting with insightful questions and suggestions to strengthen their plea for an extension and shift of proceedings.

On the next day, at 10 AM, Riya's father, Parminder and the legal team gathered at the Mumbai court for the crucial hearing. The courtroom was filled with a sense of anticipation and tension as they awaited the proceedings to begin. The court was adorned with polished wooden furniture and large, imposing portraits of past judges, representing the rich history of the Indian legal system. The room was well-lit, with sunlight streaming through large windows, casting a solemn atmosphere over the proceedings. Siddharth Malhotra, the lead lawyer, exuded confidence and determination as he prepared to present Parminder's case. Dressed in a tailored black suit, he stood at the front of the courtroom, ready to defend his client with firm dedication. The judge, adorned in a traditional black robe, entered the courtroom, commanding respect and authority. The room fell silent as everyone rose to their feet, acknowledging the presence of the court. The judge took his seat, and the proceedings commenced.

Siddharth meticulously presented his arguments, methodically dismantling the prosecution's case piece by piece. He eloquently spoke, weaving a compelling narrative that aimed to prove Parminder's innocence beyond a reasonable doubt. With each word, he exuded confidence, backed by his extensive knowledge of the law and his impressive track record. The prosecution, represented by a formidable lawyer, fiercely challenged Siddharth's arguments, attempting to poke holes in the defence's case. The courtroom was filled with intense debates, objections, and counterarguments, as both sides passionately fought for their respective positions.

Riya's father and Parminder sat in the gallery, anxiously observing the proceedings. Their hearts raced with every argument made, hoping that justice would prevail and the truth would emerge. Their eyes occasionally met Siddharth's, seeking reassurance and finding solace in his determination. As the hearing progressed, witnesses were called to testify, providing crucial pieces of evidence and shedding light on the truth of the matter. Siddharth skilfully cross-examined each witness, extracting the information that would support Parminder's defence. The courtroom drama continued for hours, with intense back-

and-forth exchanges between the defence and the prosecution.

Despite the efforts made by Siddharth and the legal team to file the necessary request for more time, their plea was met with disappointment as the court denied the extension. The gravity of the situation became even more apparent as the court ordered the immediate arrest of Parminder. The news struck like a thunderbolt, leaving the Riya's father, Parminder and the legal team in a state of shock and disbelief. They had hoped for more time to gather the evidence that would prove Parminder's innocence and prevent his arrest. However, the denial of the request meant that they had to act swiftly and come up with a new strategy to protect Parminder. In addition to the denial of the request for more time, the family and legal team faced another setback as their plea to transfer the legal proceedings to the Delhi court was also denied. The case was to be heard in the Mumbai court, which posed further challenges for the defence strategy.

Siddharth Malhotra, the experienced lawyer and partner in the firm, felt a mix of frustration, disappointment, and determination upon hearing the court's decisions. As a lawyer, he understood the importance of time and the need for a fair trial to gather evidence and present a strong defense. The denial of the extension and the transfer of proceedings meant that the time was now limited, and the odds were stacked against them. Siddharth empathized with Riya's father and felt a deep sense of responsibility to protect Parminder and ensure justice prevailed. He knew the devastating impact the arrest and the impending legal battle would have on the family. Siddharth was determined to exhaust every possible legal avenue to safeguard Parminder's rights and prove his innocence.

Parminder, on the other hand, felt a profound sense

of loss and helplessness. The denial of the requests for more time and the transfer of proceedings felt like a double blow, leaving him vulnerable to immediate arrest and unsure of his future. He experienced a whirlwind of emotions—fear, anger, and frustration—as he grappled with the reality of the situation. Parminder had never imagined himself in such a precarious position, and the weight of the consequences of losing both applications weighed heavily on him.

Despite the setbacks, Siddharth, Riya's father, and Parminder remained resolute. They understood that they had to stay strong and focus on their legal strategy moving forward. They knew that they had a tough battle ahead, but they were determined to fight for justice, challenge the accusations against Parminder, and uncover the truth that would prove his innocence. For a minute there was this total silence between 3 of them and they stand still.

As Siddharth, Riya's father, and Parminder exited the courtroom, the weight of the court's decisions hung heavily in the air. The tension was palpable as they gathered outside, seeking solace and discussing their next steps.

Siddharth: (with determination) We knew this would be a challenging battle, but we can't lose hope. We need to regroup and devise a new strategy to counter this setback.

Riya's Father: (frustrated) I can't believe they denied our requests. Parminder's arrest is imminent, and we have limited time to gather the evidence we need.

Parminder: (anxious) What are our options now? Is there anything else we can do to prevent my arrest?

Siddharth: (assuringly) No, but we won't give up, Parminder. We will explore all legal avenues available to us. We'll file an appeal and seek a stay on the arrest warrant while we gather more evidence. We'll also intensify our efforts to uncover the truth and expose those behind this conspiracy.

Riya's Father: (determined) Siddharth, we trust your expertise. Please do everything in your power to protect my son. We will support you every step of the way.

Siddharth: (grateful) Thank you for your trust. We'll work tirelessly to defend Parminder's innocence. We must stay strong and united throughout this ordeal.

Parminder: (resolved) I never anticipated facing such a situation, but I won't let it define me. I believe in our legal team, and I know we will overcome this injustice.

Siddharth: (firmly) Remember, we're in this together. We'll leave no stone unturned, and we'll fight with every resource at our disposal. We'll turn the tables and prove your innocence.

Riya's Father: (with conviction) We won't let them destroy our family. We'll emerge stronger from this, and the truth will prevail.

As Parminder was taken into custody, Riya's father stood there, his spirit crushed and his heart heavy with anguish. The weight of the situation bore down on him, leaving him feeling utterly helpless. Tears welled up in his eyes as he watched Parminder being held by one of the policemen, the realization of the loss sinking in.

Father: (voice trembling) Parminder, my son, I'm so sorry. I tried my best to protect you, but I couldn't stop this injustice. (tears stream down his face)

Father: (voice filled with regret) I should have done more, should have found a way to prevent this. I promised to keep you safe, and now... (his voice trails off, overcome by grief)

Parminder: (firmly) Father, you did everything you could. We couldn't have foreseen this. Remember, I believe in you, and I trust Siddharth and the legal team to fight for justice. We will get through this, I promise.

Father: struggling to hold back tears.

Parminder: (looking into his father's eyes) I know you Father. Your love and support mean everything to me. Remember, I'm innocent.

Father: (clenching his fists) We won't rest until the truth prevails. Our bond, our determination will guide us through this darkness. Stay strong, my son. We'll face this head-on, side by side.

As Parminder was escorted towards the police van, both father and son exchanged a glance filled with love, resilience, and belief in their fight for justice. Though their hearts were heavy with sorrow, their resolve to fight for the truth remained unbroken. They knew the road ahead would be difficult, but their bond and determination would carry them forward. Riya's father, feeling defeated and overwhelmed by the outcome of the court proceedings, dialled Riya's number, longing for some solace in this trying time. The phone rang, and Riya answered, sensing the heaviness in her father's voice.

Father: (voice filled with sorrow) Riya, it's me. I... I don't know where to begin. It didn't go well in court. They denied our request for more time, and Parminder... he has been taken into custody.

Riya: (concerned) Oh no, Dad. I can hear it in your voice. How did this happen? What are we going to do?

Father: (voice quivering) They didn't give us a chance, Riya. It feels like everything is slipping through our fingers. The court refused to transfer the proceedings to Delhi, and now Parminder... he's in custody. I feel so powerless, so defeated.

Riya: (voice filled with determination) Dad, we can't lose hope now. We have to keep fighting. We'll find another way, another strategy. We won't give up on Parminder.

Father: (sighs) I know, Riya. I know we can't give up, but it's just... it's so hard to see my son being taken away like this. I failed to protect him.

Riya: (assuringly) Dad, this is not your fault. You've done everything in your power to fight for Parminder. We'll find a way to prove his innocence, to expose the truth. We won't let him down.

Father: (voice filled with gratitude) Riya. Your words give me strength. We need to regroup, consult with the legal team, and come up with a new plan. We won't let this setback break us.

Riya: (firmly) Absolutely, Dad. We're in this together. I'll be there soon, and we'll face this head-on. Stay strong, and remember that Parminder is innocent. We will fight for justice, no matter how long it takes.

Father: (with a hint of hope) Yes, we will fight. We won't let injustice prevail.

Riya: (with determination) We're a team, Dad. We'll navigate through this storm together. Stay strong, and don't lose faith. We'll get through this and bring Parminder back home.

The phone call ended, but their unshakeable commitment to each other and their shared determination to fight for Parminder's innocence remained. Though the road ahead seemed challenging, they clung to hope, ready to face whatever obstacles came their way.

Riya: (voice filled with sadness turn towards her mom) Mom, please sit down. I need to talk to you about something... something that has happened today.

Mother: (concerned) What is it, Riya? You look so worried. What's going on?

Riya: (takes a deep breath) Mom, today in court... they... they arrested Parminder. They denied our request for more time, and he's now in custody.

Mother: (shocked and trembling) What?! How... how did this happen? I can't believe it. What about my son? Why did they arrested him?

Riya: (teary-eyed) I know, Mom, it's hard to accept. They refused to transfer the case to Delhi, and now Parminder is being held by the authorities. Dad is devastated, and we're all feeling helpless.

Mother: (voice trembling with disbelief) This can't be happening. Parminder... he's innocent. How can they do this to our family? How will Parminder stay in jail?

Riya: (reassuringly) Mom, we can't lose hope.

Mother: (tears streaming down her face) I can't bear to see my son suffer like this. What about his future, his dreams? How will we explain this to our relatives and friends?

Riya: (holding her mother's hand tightly) Mom, we have to stay strong for Parminder. We'll face this together, as a family. We won't let this situation define us. We'll fight for him, and we'll find the truth.

Mother: (voice filled with determination) You're right, Riya. Our family has always stood strong in the face of adversity. We won't let this break us. We'll support Parminder, and we'll do whatever it takes to bring him back home.

Riya and her mother sat there, holding each other's hands, finding solace in their shared strength and determination. As the night unfolded, Riya and her mother engaged in deep discussions, weighing their options and contemplating the next steps. They realized that being with her father in Mumbai during this challenging time was of utmost importance. Riya made the decision to travel to Mumbai immediately to offer her support and stand by her family. The following morning, Riya packed her bags, collected all related documents and information from office. She knew that her presence in Mumbai would provide emotional strength to her father, and together they could face the daunting legal battle that lay ahead. With her mother's blessings and a heavy heart, Riya bid farewell and embarked on her journey to Mumbai.

SIX

Entangled Hearts

Aug 2009

During the flight, Riya's mind was filled with a whirlwind of emotions. She reflected on the gravity of the situation and the uncertainties that awaited her in Mumbai. She knew that her family needed her now more than ever, and she was ready to shoulder the responsibility of standing alongside her father. Upon arriving in Mumbai, Riya was greeted by the bustling city and the humid air. She hailed a taxi and directed the driver to her father's location. As the taxi weaved through the streets, Riya's anticipation grew, and her heart raced with a mix of nervousness and determination.

Finally, the taxi pulled up in front of her father's residence. Riya paid the driver and hurriedly made her way to the entrance. For years, the Mumbai flat had been a constant presence in the lives of the Malhotra family. Nestled in the heart of the bustling city, it served as their haven whenever they visited Mumbai for their business ventures. She took a deep breath, gathered her strength, and rang the doorbell. The door swung open, revealing her father, who appeared tired but relieved to see his daughter. They embraced tightly, finding comfort in each other's presence. Words were not necessary at that moment, as their unspoken bond and shared understanding spoke volumes. They spent the entire evening engrossed in discussions, meticulously analyzing the matter and reviewing the documents she had gathered and brought along.

Later in the evening Riya took a moment to gather herself before making a phone call to her friend, vidya in Mumbai. She dialled the number and anxiously waited for her to answer. Vidya picked up, Riya's voice trembled as she explained the difficult situation her family was facing and why they were in Mumbai. She poured her heart out, sharing the emotional turmoil they were going through and the need for support during this challenging time. Vidya listened attentively, offering words of comfort and assurance that she would be there for Riya and her family.

After hanging up the phone, Riya took a deep breath and dialled another number. This time, it was Raj whom she called. They had been close friends for years, sharing laughter, adventures, and moments of support. As the phone rang, Riya's heart raced as she dialled Raj's number, her mind filled with a mix of anticipation and nervousness. After a few rings, Raj finally picked up the call, and his voice immediately brought a wave of comfort and familiarity.

Raj: "Hello? Riya? Is that you?"
Riya: "Yes, Raj, it's me! It's been so long since we last spoke. How have you been?"
Raj: "Oh, Riya, I can't even begin to express how glad I am to hear your voice. It feels like ages since we last caught up. I've missed our conversations."
Riya's voice filled with happiness as she replied, "I've missed them too, Raj. You have no idea how much I've wanted to share this with you. But first, how have you been? How's everything going?"

Raj chuckled softly, his warmth evident in his words. "Well, life has been keeping me busy, as usual. But I'm doing well. Now, tell me, what's on your mind?

Riya took a deep breath, the weight of her words lingering in the silence before she spoke. "Raj, I'm in Mumbai. I came to India few months back but got caught up and I wanted to talk to you because I trust you, and I know you've always been there for me. Our family business is going through a crisis, and I need your assistance. I thought talking to you would make me feel better, and perhaps you can offer some guidance too."

"Of course, Riya. I'm here for you," Raj's voice turned serious and reassuring. "I'm glad to know that you are in Mumbai. You know you can count on me. Now tell me everything, I'm listening."

Riya's voice quivered as she explained the situation, conveying the gravity of the circumstances her family was facing. She spoke about the legal battle, her father's anguish, and the need for their friendship and support during this trying time.

Raj listened attentively, his silence speaking volumes. Raj's mind was in a state of turmoil as he processed the shocking revelation he had just heard from Riya. Raj's voice trembled with a mix of confusion and disbelief as he struggled to comprehend the gravity of the situation. Finally, he managed to utter a single question that hung in the air, "Riya, what is your brother's name?" His tone revealed a sense of urgency and shock, as if a sudden realization had struck him.

Riya, taken aback by Raj's response, paused for a moment, trying to gather her thoughts. She hesitated before answering, her voice filled with uncertainty, "His name is Parminder. Why do you ask, Raj? Is something wrong?"

There was a brief silence on the other end of the line, as if Raj was trying to find the right words to express the whirlwind of emotions surging within him. Eventually, he managed to speak, his voice heavy with sorrow, "Riya, I... I need some time to process everything. I'll call you back soon."

Before Riya could respond, Raj abruptly ended the call, leaving her with a sense of unease and confusion. She held the phone in her hand, her mind racing with questions and her heart heavy with concern for both her brother and her friend. Unable to make sense of Raj's reaction, Riya decided to let it go for the moment. She knew she had to be there for her father, who needed her support now more than ever. With a mix of trepidation and determination, she made her way to her father's side, leaving the unanswered questions about Raj's cryptic response to linger in her mind.

As she sat beside her father. Her father, lost in his own world of worries and uncertainties, looked up at Riya with a somber expression. He could sense that something was troubling her, but in that moment, he lacked the words to address it. Instead, he offered a faint smile, silently acknowledging her presence and the comfort it provided. Her thoughts wandered back to the phone call with Raj. She couldn't shake off the feeling that something was amiss, but she understood that Raj needed time to process the shocking revelation about her brother. Resolving to be patient and supportive, she focused her attention on her father, hoping to provide him with the comfort and strength he needed in that moment of uncertainty.

The next morning, Riya woke up with a sense of purpose and determination. She went to her father and informed him that she was going to the legal team's office to discuss their strategy and gather updates on Parminder's case. Her father, with a gentle smile on his face, nodded in understanding. "Go ahead, my dear. Take your time at the legal team's office. But before that, why don't you visit the temple? Seek the blessings of the divine before you embark on this important journey," he suggested, his voice filled with love and concern.

Riya felt a surge of gratitude towards her father for his thoughtful suggestion. She understood the significance of seeking spiritual strength during challenging times. With a nod and a warm embrace, she assured her father that she would visit the temple before heading to the legal team's office. Leaving her home, Riya made her way to the nearby temple. The air was filled with the scent of incense, and the soft sound of devotional chants enveloped her. She stood before the divine idols, closing her eyes and offering heartfelt prayers for guidance, strength, and the well-being of her family.

In that moment of quiet reflection, Riya found solace and a renewed sense of hope. She believed that the divine would guide her steps and provide the strength she needed to face the challenges ahead. With a grateful heart, she concluded her visit to the temple and began her journey to the legal team's office. Riya, feeling slightly frustrated by the reception's refusal to let her in, turned to leave Siddharth's office. However, just as she was about to walk away, a voice called out to her from behind. She turned around to see Siddharth himself standing there, his face displaying a mix of apology and understanding. "Riya, I'm sorry for the confusion. Please come with me to my cabin," Siddharth said, gesturing for her to follow him. Surprised by his sudden appearance and his unexpected invitation, Riya's curiosity piqued, and she quickly nodded in acknowledgment. She followed Siddharth through the bustling office, past rows of desks occupied by lawyers engrossed in their work, and into his private cabin. Once inside, Siddharth motioned for Riya to take a seat and settled himself behind his desk. She couldn't help but notice the warmth and inviting ambiance of the space.

The room was tastefully decorated, reflecting Siddharth's personality and his values.
The walls were adorned with framed photographs capturing precious moments with his family, showcasing his love and respect for his parents. There were pictures of Siddharth as a child, standing proudly alongside his parents, radiating a sense of joy and togetherness. These images spoke volumes about the deep bond he shared with his family and the importance he placed on their happiness. On the corner of Siddharth's desk, there was a small wooden sculpture of a family, symbolizing his strong familial ties. It served as a constant reminder of his roots and the importance of cherishing those relationships. The sculpture was meticulously crafted, showcasing the attention to detail that Siddharth possessed in all aspects of his life.

The bookshelf in the corner of the room was lined with an array of books, covering various genres from law to literature. It reflected Siddharth's love for knowledge and his continuous pursuit of learning. The titles ranged from legal textbooks to classics, displaying his diverse interests and intellectual curiosity. A framed photograph caught Riya's eye as she glanced at the bookshelf. It was a picture of Siddharth with a group of friends, presumably from his school days. Their smiles were infectious, radiating a sense of camaraderie and shared memories. It was evident that Siddharth valued his friendships and cherished the connections he had built over the years. The room exuded a sense of calmness and organization, reflecting Siddharth's meticulous nature and attention to detail. The desk was neatly arranged, with files and legal documents stacked methodically. It showcased his professionalism and commitment to his work.

Siddharth began, his tone sincere and pull a chair to

sit next to him "I apologize for the inconvenience, Riya, I should have anticipated the need for an appointment given the circumstances. Please understand that my schedule can be quite demanding."

Riya, though still taken aback by the sudden turn of events, nodded in understanding. She appreciated Siddharth's willingness to accommodate her despite the initial confusion. "Thank you, Siddharth, for your graciousness and for accommodating me even without any prior notice,"

Siddharth acknowledged and continued, his gaze focused and attentive "Now, let's get to the matter at hand, tell me what have you got for me regarding the case and any other pertinent information, We need to act swiftly to protect him."

Riya took a deep breath, grateful for Siddharth's willingness to listen and assist. She proceeded to share the details of Parminder's case, providing him with the evidence they had gathered so far and explaining the challenges. As she spoke, Siddharth listened intently, occasionally asking clarifying questions and jotting down notes. His expressions shifted from concern to determination, reflecting his commitment to fighting for justice.

Siddharth reassured her, his voice filled with conviction "Riya, I assure you, we will do everything in our power to help your brother, I will personally oversee the proceedings and assemble a strong legal team to advocate for Parminder's innocence." As Siddharth observed the sadness and despair on Riya's face, he couldn't help but feel a profound sense of sorrow and guilt. He understood the weight of the situation and the impact it had on her and her family. In an attempt to provide some comfort, he offered her a cup of coffee, hoping to create a moment of normalcy amidst the chaos.

Siddharth asked gently, his voice filled with empathy "Riya, would you like some coffee?" However, Riya's response was distant and unresponsive. Her mind was preoccupied with the distressing circumstances surrounding her brother and the uncertain future they faced. The offer of coffee seemed insignificant in comparison to the gravity of the situation. Undeterred, Siddharth attempted to initiate a casual conversation, asking about the well-being of her mother and other family members. He hoped that discussing familiar topics might provide a temporary respite from the overwhelming stress they were all experiencing. "How is your mother doing, Riya? And the rest of your family?" Siddharth inquired, his voice sincere and compassionate.

Riya's gaze softened as she appreciated Siddharth's concern for her family's well-being. She took a moment to gather her thoughts before responding. "They are all struggling with the situation, Siddharth," Riya replied, her voice tinged with a mix of sadness and exhaustion. "My mother is trying to stay strong, but it's taking a toll on her. We are all doing our best to support each other during this difficult time."

Siddharth nodded understandingly, recognizing the immense emotional burden they carried. He knew that offering legal assistance was only part of the battle; providing empathy and support during such trying times was equally important.

Siddharth said softly "I understand, Riya, Please let your family know that they have my deepest sympathies and that I am here for them as well. We will do everything we can to navigate this challenging situation together."

Riya appreciated Siddharth's genuine concern and

compassion. She acknowledged his words with a grateful nod, recognizing that they were not alone in their fight for justice. Siddharth continued: So, Riya, tell me about your work and qualifications. I'm curious to know more about your expertise in international trade and law practices.

Riya: Thank you, Siddharth. I have always been passionate about international trade and its legal implications. I pursued a degree in International Trade Law and gained practical experience through internships and working with multinational companies. It's a constantly evolving field, and I enjoy staying updated on the latest developments.

Siddharth: That's impressive, Riya. International trade is a fascinating area, and it's crucial to understand the legal aspects to ensure fair and ethical practices. I'm intrigued to know what's happening in other parts of the world, especially when it comes to trade policies and regulations.

Riya: Absolutely! The global landscape is constantly changing, and trade relations play a significant role in shaping economies. It's essential to stay informed about international trade agreements, disputes, and emerging markets. I believe that understanding these dynamics can provide valuable insights and help businesses navigate complex legal landscapes.

Siddharth: You have a unique perspective, Riya. It's refreshing to hear your passion and knowledge in this field. By exploring different perspectives and understanding diverse legal systems, we can broaden our horizons and bring new insights to our clients.

Riya: I completely agree, Siddharth. It's crucial to have a global mindset and be well-versed in various legal frameworks. It allows us to approach cases from different angles and provide comprehensive solutions.

Siddharth: Time has flown by, and I must say, our conversation has been enlightening. By the way, Riya, have you had the chance to explore Mumbai before?

Riya: No, Siddharth. I've heard so much about its vibrant culture and bustling streets. I would love to explore the city but when the time is right.

Siddharth: Well, Riya, I can't let you leave Mumbai without experiencing its charm. How about we take some time off and go on a mini-tour? I'll show you some of the city's hidden gems and give you a taste of its rich heritage.

Riya: That sounds wonderful, Siddharth. I would be delighted to explore Mumbai with someone who knows the city well. It's a generous offer, and I can't thank you enough. But..

Siddharth: Consider it my way of welcoming you to Mumbai and offering a small respite from the challenges you and your family are facing. We all need moments of joy amidst the storm.

Riya: Thank you, Siddharth. Your kindness means a lot to me and my family. I look forward.

Siddharth accompanied Riya downstairs. They exchanged a few more pleasantries before Riya hailed a cab to head back home. Siddharth watched as the cab pulled away, his thoughts filled with a mix of admiration and concern for Riya and her family. As the cab drove through the bustling streets of Mumbai, Riya couldn't help but replay the events of the day in her mind. The conversation with Siddharth had brought a sense of comfort and understanding amidst the chaos surrounding her family's situation. She appreciated his empathy and genuine interest in her well-being.

As Riya settled into the cab, she reached for her phone and dialled Raj's number, hoping to connect with him and share the events of her day. However, her attempts went unanswered, and a tinge of concern crept into her thoughts. She wondered if something was amiss or if

Raj was preoccupied with his own responsibilities. Setting aside her worries for the moment, Riya decided to meet her friend Vidya for dinner. Vidya has always been her pillar of support, a constant presence in her life, and Riya knew that spending time with her would provide some much-needed solace and distraction from the recent turmoil.

Vidya is a spirited, bold and passionate individual with a strong sense of purpose. From an early age, she was driven by a desire to fight for what is right and to be a voice for those who couldn't speak up for themselves. This sense of justice and advocacy led her to pursue a career in law, where she initially believed she could make a difference in the courtroom. However, her path took a turn when she discovered her true calling in journalism. As a fearless journalist, Vidya possesses a sharp and analytical mind. She has a keen eye for details and an insatiable curiosity to get to the heart of every story. Her determination to seek the truth is matched only by her exceptional investigative skills. Vidya is not one to back down from tough assignments or dangerous situations, as she believes that it is her duty to shine a light on issues that need to be addressed. Her commitment to her work is unwavering, and she takes immense pride in her role as a journalist.

Vidya firmly believes that writing and talking about certain things can bring change in society and in people's lives. Her passion for her profession is fuelled by a deep-seated belief in the power of words and the potential they hold to create a positive impact on the world. Beyond her professional persona, Vidya is a warm and caring individual, fiercely loyal to her friends and family. Riya had a few relationships in the past, but they didn't last for long. Her bond with Riya is a testament to the depth of her friendships, and she is always ready to offer support and encouragement to those she cares about. Despite her serious and tenacious nature as a journalist, Vidya also has a playful and fun side, which she reveals to those close to her. Growing up in a family dedicated to public service, Vidya imbibed the values of integrity, honesty, and courage from her father, the IPS officer. She admires his dedication to serving the public and strives to emulate his commitment to making a positive impact on society through her work.

Riya and Vidya met at a cozy restaurant, their conversation filled with laughter and reminiscing about old times. Over a delicious meal, they delved into various topics, ranging from their shared dreams and aspirations to the challenges they faced in their respective journeys. Vidya's positive energy and support uplifted Riya's spirits, reminding her of the importance of friendship and the strength it brings during difficult times.

Riya: Thank you so much for dinner, Vidya. It was great catching up with you after such a long time.

Vidya: You're welcome, Riya. I'm glad we could spend some time together and take your mind off things for a while.

Riya: It's been a tough day, Vidya. The situation with my family is still uncertain, and it's taking a toll on all of us. But I'm trying to stay strong and hopeful. I know we'll find a way through this.

Vidya: I admire your strength, Riya. I can only imagine how challenging it must be for you. Just know that I'm here for you, no matter what. You're not alone in this.

Riya: Vidya, it's so good to see you. It feels like ages since we last caught up. How's life been treating you in Mumbai?

Vidya: Riya, it's great to see you too! Life in Mumbai has been both exciting and challenging. The city has so much to offer, but it can be quite overwhelming at times. How about you? How's was new York?

Riya: Well, New York was an incredible experience. I was working on some exciting projects and building a life there. But now, I'm back in Mumbai, trying to navigate through these challenging times. My family is going through a tough situation, and I had to rush back from New York to be with them. It's been quite a rollercoaster ride.

Vidya: I understand Riya, and I'm so sorry to hear that. If there's anything I can do to help, please let me know.

Riya: Thank you, Vidya. Your support means a lot to me. It's times like these that remind us of the true value of friendship. Speaking of which, I tried calling Raj earlier, but he didn't answer.

Vidya: I'm sorry, Riya, I hope he's okay.

Riya: That's worrying. I hope he's just caught up with something and nothing serious. I'll keep trying to reach out to him. Maybe I'll text him later and see if he responds.

Vidya: That sounds like a good plan, Riya. Hopefully, he'll get back to you soon. In the meantime, focus on taking care of yourself and your family. We're all here for you, and things will get better.

Riya: Thank you, Vidya. Your words of encouragement mean a lot to me. Let's stay in touch and keep each other updated. We'll face these challenges together, and I'm grateful to have you by my side.

Vidya: Riya, you don't have to thank me. We've been friends for so long, and supporting each other is what friends do. I want you to know that I'll be there in every court hearing, standing with you and your family. We'll face this together.

Riya: Your presence in court will bring us immense strength and courage. Knowing that you're standing by our side means the world to us. And your expertise as a journalist, I truly appreciate your willingness to investigate this matter and tell our side of the story. It's crucial that the truth comes out.

Vidya: Riya, as a journalist, I have a responsibility to seek the truth and bring justice to light. I'll make this case a top priority and work tirelessly to uncover any hidden agendas. The public deserves to know the facts, and I'll do my best to ensure our side is heard.

Riya: Vidya, I can't thank you enough for your determination and support. You're not just a dear friend but also a ray of hope in these challenging times. Your promise to investigate and print the story means so much to me. I trust your skills and integrity. Riya was almost in tears and hugged Vidya. Vidya dropped Riya off at her home and met her father and bid him farewell.

As Riya entered her room, she decided to unwind and find solace in music. She turned on her favourite playlist, letting the soothing melodies envelop her. The music acted as a comforting lullaby, gradually easing her worries and stress. The gentle tunes filled the room, creating a peaceful atmosphere. Lying on her bed, Riya closed her eyes, letting the music transport her to a place of tranquillity. The melodic rhythms and soulful lyrics resonated with her emotions, helping her to find a sense of calm amidst the storm. With each passing song, her mind began to drift away, and the weight of the day's events slowly faded. As the melodies continued to play softly in the background, Riya's body and mind began to relax. The stress and tension of the day melted away, and a sense of serenity washed over her. Gradually, sleep embraced her, carrying her into a peaceful slumber.

Next morning, Siddharth arrived at Riya's doorstep, ready for their day out in Mumbai. Riya eagerly greeted him with a warm smile, feeling a sense of excitement and anticipation for the adventures that lay ahead. Riya, with her inherent grace and natural beauty, chose to wear a white outfit adorned with a pink dupatta for her day out in Mumbai with Siddharth. Her white ensemble, perhaps reflecting her desire for purity and innocence amidst the turmoil surrounding her family, was complemented perfectly by the delicate touch of the pink dupatta. Riya's hair was neatly tied back in a tight hairstyle, allowing her facial features to shine and giving her a polished and sophisticated look. The simplicity of her hairstyle emphasized her natural beauty, accentuating her expressive eyes and radiant smile. To complete her ensemble, Riya adorned herself with oxidized ornaments, which added a touch of traditional charm and a sense of heritage to her overall appearance. The intricate designs and antique finish of the jewellery reflected her appreciation for craftsmanship and tradition.

Her choice of attire and accessories exuded a sense of understated elegance and refined taste. While her outfit and styling reflected simplicity, they also represented her individuality and the unique blend of grace and beauty that she possessed. In the midst of her family's legal battle, Riya's choice to embrace grace and beauty with simplicity was a testament to her character and inner resolve. It spoke volumes about her ability to find strength and beauty in the midst of adversity, embodying the idea that true beauty comes from within.

As Siddharth laid eyes on Riya in her elegant white outfit with a pink dupatta, he couldn't help but be captivated by her beauty. It was as if he was seeing her in a whole new light, appreciating her grace and charm in a way he hadn't before. He found himself wondering why he hadn't noticed her beauty earlier, perhaps blinded by the weight of the circumstances that had brought them together. In that moment, Riya's radiance and simplicity struck a chord within him, drawing him closer to her.

Siddharth couldn't help but feel a sense of attraction towards Riya, not just for her external beauty but also for the strength and resilience she displayed in the face of adversity. Her grace and poise in the midst of challenging times showcased her inner beauty and made him realize the depth of her character. He silently contemplated how he had overlooked the qualities that now seemed so apparent to him. Siddharth found himself intrigued by Riya's presence and felt a growing desire to explore their connection further.

In that moment, Siddharth began to see Riya in a different light, recognizing the unique combination of grace, beauty, and strength she possessed. He couldn't help but be drawn to her, wanting to know more about the person beneath the surface and explore the potential for a deeper connection. Siddharth, looking dashing as always, stepped out of the car and walked around to open the door for Riya. With a warm smile, he gestured for her to enter the car, taking care of every detail to make her feel special. Riya graciously accepted his gesture, her movements exuding elegance as she settled herself in the car. Siddharth had planned a full day of exploration and discovery. He suggested starting their city tour by visiting iconic landmarks such as the Gateway of India and Marine Drive, where they could take a leisurely stroll along the picturesque promenade. Riya agreed enthusiastically, eager to immerse herself in the vibrant energy of Mumbai.

As they made their way through the bustling streets of the city, Siddharth shared interesting anecdotes and trivia about the history, culture, and significance of each place they visited. Riya found herself captivated by his knowledge and passion, as well as his ability to make every moment feel special. Their next stop was the famous Chhatrapati Shivaji Terminus, a magnificent railway station that showcased the architectural grandeur of Mumbai. They marvelled at the intricate details of the structure and soaked in the lively atmosphere, surrounded by the hustle and bustle of commuters and travellers. Siddharth, being the perfect host, made sure to treat Riya to some authentic Mumbai street food. They savoured mouth-watering *Vada pav, Pav bhaji, Sandwiches, Malai Kulfi* and other local delicacies, relishing the flavours that Mumbai was renowned for. The day continued with visits to popular markets like Colaba Causeway and Linking Road, where they indulged in some retail therapy, browsing through an array of trendy fashion boutiques and unique street stalls. Siddharth's keen eye for fashion and style guided Riya in selecting a few special items that caught her eye. As the day drew to a close, they found themselves at Bandstand, enjoying the stunning sunset and the gentle waves of the Arabian Sea. They sat on the sandy shore, engaging in heartfelt conversations and sharing moments of laughter and joy. The peaceful ambiance provided the perfect backdrop for their connection to grow stronger.

As the sun dipped below the horizon, Siddharth dropped Riya back home, both of them feeling a deep sense of contentment and gratitude for the memorable day they had spent together. Riya thanked Siddharth for his companionship and for creating such wonderful memories. They bid each other farewell, looking forward to the next chapter of their journey, both as friends and allies in the fight for justice.

During the three months that Riya's father was in Mumbai, her mother and other family members took on the responsibility of managing the family business and household affairs back home in Delhi. It was a challenging time for them, but they understood the importance of supporting Riya and her father during the legal battle. Riya's mother, being a capable and strong-willed woman, stepped up to ensure that everything ran smoothly in her husband's absence. She coordinated with the employees and handled the day-to-day operations of the business with utmost dedication and efficiency. Her leadership skills and ability to make critical decisions were instrumental in maintaining the stability of the business during this trying period.

In addition to managing the business, Riya's mother also took care of the household responsibilities with the support of other family members. They worked together, creating a sense of unity and strength amidst the challenges. Despite the distance, Riya's father remained in constant communication, providing emotional support and guidance. Trusted employees and family friends also offered their assistance, easing the burden on Riya's mother and allowing her to focus on supporting the family.

As the legal battle progressed and Riya started working with Siddharth's legal team, her father began to consider returning to Delhi. Realizing the critical situation, he faced a tough decision. While he wanted to be there for Riya and Parminder, he also understood the urgency of overseeing the family business and supporting his wife. The showroom's financial and reputational challenges needed his immediate attention. Riya's mother had been single-handedly managing everything for months, and it was becoming overwhelming for her. He knew that finding a solution to maintain the showroom's success and reputation was crucial for the family's well-being. With the understanding and agreement of Riya and Siddharth, Riya's father made the decision to return to Delhi. He had full faith in Siddharth and the legal team's ability to handle the case effectively, and he believed that his presence was crucial to ensure the smooth functioning of their business and provide support to his wife.

Before leaving, Riya's father had a heartfelt conversation with Riya, expressing his love and pride in her for standing determined for family. He assured her that he would always be there for her, no matter the distance, and encouraged her to stay strong and have faith in the legal process. Riya, in turn, assured her father that she would continue fighting for justice and make him proud. Father also spoke to Vidya and Siddharth for the support. As Riya's father returned home, the family once again united, working together to overcome the challenges they faced. Throughout this time, the bond between Riya's parents grew even stronger. They demonstrated resilience, trust, and mutual respect, setting an example for their children on how to face adversity with courage and unity. The love and support they provided to each other.

SEVEN

The fight for justice

————◦ₚ◦————

During the six-month wait for the next hearing, Siddharth's legal team made several attempts to secure bail for Parminder. However, they faced multiple rejections from the court due to the gravity of the charges against him, which involved serious fraud and money laundering. The defense lawyer argued diligently, presenting various grounds for bail, but the court deemed it inappropriate given the nature of the case and the potential risks associated with releasing Parminder. The court, taking into consideration the evidence presented by the prosecution and the severity of the allegations, emphasized the need to ensure the accused's presence during the trial. The judge cited concerns about the possibility of Parminder tampering with evidence or influencing witnesses if granted bail. As a result, the court deemed it necessary to keep him in custody until the trial proceedings were completed.

Siddharth saw the potential in Riya's skills and expertise and offered her a freelancing opportunity in his office. Recognizing her talent and dedication, he wanted to utilize her abilities to contribute to the expansion of his firm. Siddharth had been contemplating the establishment of an additional division within his firm, and he believed that Riya's expertise and fresh perspective would be valuable in this endeavour. He saw her as a capable and resourceful professional who could bring new ideas and insights to the table.

Riya, grateful for the opportunity, enthusiastically accepted the offer. Being alone in Mumbai and fighting for her brother, she felt it would be a great experience, as she had been spending her days going to court and meeting Parminder in jail from time to time, with not much else to do. She began working closely with Siddharth and his team, immersing herself in the project and providing valuable input. Her international trade and law practices background proved to be instrumental in shaping the new division's framework. Under Siddharth's guidance and mentorship, Riya thrived in her role as a consultant. She demonstrated a keen understanding of the business dynamics and showcased her ability to adapt to new challenges. Her dedication, hard work, and innovative thinking quickly gained recognition within the firm. As the months passed, Riya's contributions to the new division became increasingly significant. Her strong work ethic and passion for her craft helped accelerate the progress of the project. Siddharth, impressed by her professionalism and commitment, valued her as an integral part of the team.

One afternoon, Riya noticed a familiar face entering Siddharth's room. He was a tall, charming guy whom she had met previously at her friend's birthday party. Intrigued and surprised, Riya's curiosity got the better of her, and she decided to stop him before he could leave. With a friendly smile, Riya approached him and said, "Hey, excuse me! I think we've met before at a friend's birthday party, right? Rohan, I guess?"

"Oh, yes! I remember you now. You're Riya, right? It's great to see you again."

His initial recognition and smile quickly faded, and he seemed reluctant to acknowledge her presence. It was evident that something was bothering him, and he appeared determined to distance himself from Riya. she was taken aback by his sudden change in demeanour. Riya nodded, feeling a mix of excitement and curiosity.

"Yes, that's me. It's a pleasant surprise to see you here. What brings you to Siddharth's office?"
He started to explain that he had been working with Siddharth on a project. He mentioned that he had recently joined the team and was collaborating closely with Siddharth on various business matters. Intrigued by Rohan's presence, Riya couldn't help but ask, "So, how do you know Siddharth? Are you friends?"

Rohan chuckled and replied, "Actually, Siddharth and I go way back. We were childhood friends and schoolmates. We lost touch for a while, but fate brought us back together when we realized our professional paths aligned. It's been great working with him and he left"

Riya was amazed by the connection between Siddharth and Rohan. She found it fascinating how their paths had crossed once again, this time in a professional setting. It made her reflect on the mysterious ways in which life brings people together. While Riya didn't know it at the time, this chance encounter with Rohan would play a significant role in her life and the unfolding of her story. The reconnection between Siddharth, Riya, and Rohan would create a dynamic bond and influence the course of events in unexpected ways.

Riya couldn't shake off the nagging feeling about Rohan and the unexpected encounter in Siddharth's office. Determined to find some answers, she mustered the courage to approach Siddharth and inquire about their connection. She knew it was not her place to pry into Siddharth's personal matters, but her curiosity and intuition urged her to seek some clarity. Taking a deep breath, Riya knocked on Siddharth's office door and entered when he beckoned her in. Siddharth looked up from his work, noticing the seriousness on Riya's face. Sensing her unease, he gestured for her to sit down.

"Siddharth, I hope you don't mind me asking, but I noticed Rohan in your office earlier. We've met before, and it seemed like he didn't want to acknowledge me. Do you know him well?" Riya inquired, her voice filled with curiosity and concern. Siddharth paused for a moment, a hint of contemplation in his eyes. He understood Riya's need for answers and decided to be honest with her. "Riya, Rohan is an old friend of mine. We used to be close during our school days. However, something happened between us, and we drifted apart. It's a complicated story, and I haven't seen him in years." Riya listened attentively, her mind racing with questions. She sensed that there was more to the story than Siddharth was letting on. "Is there a reason he seemed so distant and reluctant to talk to me? Did something happen between us that I'm not aware of?"

Siddharth sighed, his gaze fixed on a distant point. "Riya, I can't speak for Rohan's actions or emotions. Whatever transpired between you two is something I'm not privy to. People change, circumstances change, and sometimes, friendships take unexpected turns. I'm sorry I can't provide you with more clarity on this matter."

Riya nodded, understanding that there were certain boundaries Siddharth couldn't breach. She respected his honesty and realized that some things were beyond her control. Little did Riya know that this encounter was just the beginning of a series of revelations that would reshape her understanding of the past and challenge her perception of the present. The journey to uncover the truth would take her on unexpected paths, testing her resilience and pushing the boundaries of her relationships.

As she returned to her work, Riya couldn't help but wonder what secrets and hidden connections lay beneath the surface. She remained determined to embrace the unknown, ready to face whatever revelations awaited her in the days to come. She couldn't shake off the nagging suspicion that something was amiss. The encounters with both Raj and Rohan had left her bewildered and confused. There seemed to be a pattern, a puzzle she couldn't quite decipher. Unable to keep her thoughts to herself, Riya reached out to her trusted friend, Vidya. She recounted the incidents, explaining her concerns and the connections she was trying to make. But instead of sharing her worries, Vidya simply laughed off Riya's suspicions, dismissing them as mere imagination.

Vidya said playfully "Come on, Riya, You're letting your imagination run wild. Sometimes things are just coincidences. Don't overthink it."

Though Riya appreciated Vidya's attempt to alleviate her concerns, she couldn't shake off the feeling that there was more to the story. Deep down, she knew she couldn't ignore these strange encounters. Her gut feeling told her that there was a hidden link that needed to be unravelled. Vidya, understanding Riya's persistence and knowing her well, sensed that there might be something deeper at play. She paused for a moment and then changed her tone.

Vidya said with a more serious tone "Okay, Riya, I trust your instincts, let's discuss and investigate it further. Before we proceed, I wanted to share that I've come across some information that might shed some light on your brother's case. But I need to meet you in person to share it with you."

Riya's eyes widened with a mix of curiosity and hope. She knew Vidya wouldn't make such claims lightly. It was evident that Vidya had stumbled upon something significant, something that could potentially turn the tide in their favour.

Riya responded eagerly, "Let's meet as soon as possible".
Vidya agreed "We need to tread carefully and ensure utmost secrecy. I'll find a secure location where we can discuss this in detail." emphasizing the need for caution. She stressed that the information she had was sensitive and needed to be handled discreetly. They decided on a meeting place away from prying eyes, where they could freely discuss their findings and plan their next steps. Riya hung up the phone, a mix of excitement and apprehension filled her.

Riya and Vidya agreed to meet in a discreet and secure location, away from prying eyes. They chose a small, cozy cafe tucked away in a quiet corner of the city. As Riya entered the cafe, she noticed Vidya sitting at a secluded table near the back. The air was thick with anticipation as Riya approached Vidya. Vidya greeted her with a serious expression, indicating the gravity of the information she possessed. Without wasting any time, Vidya handed over a folder containing a stack of documents. The folder was unmarked, a subtle indication of the sensitive nature of its contents.

Riya's heart raced with a mixture of excitement and nervousness as she opened the folder. The documents revealed a complex web of financial transactions, offshore accounts, and shell companies. It became evident that several powerful and popular politicians and businessmen were involved in a vast network of money laundering and illicit activities. Page after page, Riya discovered evidence of fraudulent transactions, manipulated financial records, and the creation of fake companies to facilitate illegal activities. The names of influential individuals were splattered across the documents, raising questions about their integrity and involvement in criminal acts.

As Riya delved deeper into the documents, she stumbled upon a series of transactions linking these powerful figures to her brother's case. It became clear that their actions were not only jeopardizing her brother's life but also exploiting innocent people and tarnishing the system. However, amidst the revelations, there was one missing piece in the puzzle that continued to haunt Riya. The mention of this person's name and their sudden disappearance added a layer of intrigue and suspense to the unfolding story.

Riya and Vidya exchanged glances, their determination growing stronger with each passing moment. They understood the magnitude of the information they possessed and the risks involved in exposing the truth. But they were fuelled by a shared sense of justice and a deep desire to bring down the corrupt individuals who had wreaked havoc on innocent lives. Riya and Vidya knew that the documents they had obtained were crucial evidence that needed to be verified and presented to the legal team, as well as Siddharth. However, they were concerned about the acceptance of these documents in court, especially since they couldn't disclose the identity of the source who had provided them.

Unable to reach Siddharth over the phone, Riya decided that they would meet him in person to discuss the situation. They scheduled a meeting for the next day in Siddharth's office, hoping that he would be available to provide guidance and advice. Riya anxiously dialled Siddharth's number, hoping that he would answer this time. However, to her disappointment, the call went unanswered.

Next day morning, Riya was getting ready to meet Siddharth at his office when she heard the doorbell ring.

Surprised by the unexpected visit, she hurriedly went to answer the door. To her astonishment, it was Siddharth standing right outside her home. With a warm smile, Riya welcomed Siddharth inside and invited him to have a seat. She offered him a cup of tea, wanting to make him feel comfortable. Siddharth thanked her for the hospitality and accepted the offer, appreciating the gesture. As Riya prepared the tea, she couldn't help but wonder why Siddharth had come to her place instead of meeting at the office as planned. She was curious to find out the reason behind his visit and hoped that it was something important related to their ongoing discussions.

Once the tea was ready, Riya served it to Siddharth and they settled down for a conversation. She couldn't contain her curiosity any longer and asked, "Siddharth," Riya began, her voice tinged with both anticipation and a hint of hesitation, "I did call you last night because there was something crucial I wanted to share with you. However, before I reveal that, I'm curious to know why you're here so early in the morning. Is there a specific reason for your visit?"

Siddharth paused for a moment, collecting his thoughts. He knew he had to be honest with Riya and explain the situation clearly. With a composed yet serious expression, he responded, "Riya, I came here this morning because I received some information overnight that could significantly impact our case. It's vital that we discuss it in person before our scheduled meeting at the office."

Riya's eyes widened in anticipation, her curiosity piqued even further. Siddharth continued, "The information I received sheds new light on the case and provides valuable insights into the truth behind the corruption and illicit activities we've been investigating. It's crucial that we go through it together, verify its authenticity, and decide on the appropriate course of action."

Riya's mind raced with possibilities, trying to connect the dots between the information she had received and Siddharth's visit. It became evident that their paths were converging, and the pieces of the puzzle were falling into place. Realizing the importance of the moment, Riya nodded in understanding. "I see," she said, her voice filled with determination. "It seems like our paths are aligning, Siddharth. I believe the information I received might complement what you've just shared. We need to collaborate, verify the details, and present a strong case to the legal team."

Siddharth listened attentively as Riya explained the source of the documents she possessed. He couldn't help but feel a mix of surprise and admiration for Riya's resourcefulness and her friend Vidya's involvement. The timing of their discoveries and the alignment of their efforts raised a few suspicions in Siddharth's mind.

Siddharth said with curiosity "Vidya, I've heard about her, your journalist friend. It seems like she has been working diligently behind the scenes, gathering evidence to support our case. I must say, Riya, you have an excellent team cum friend by your side."

Riya nodded, acknowledging Vidya's dedication and the risks she had taken to uncover the truth. "Yes, Vidya has been discreetly investigating and gathering information from her sources. She believes that exposing the corrupt individuals involved in this case is not only crucial for justice but also for the greater good of society."

Siddharth's curiosity grew, and he couldn't help but ask, "Do we have any insights into the identity of the person who provided these documents to Vidya? It's essential for us to know if the source can be trusted and if the information is reliable."

Riya paused for a moment, contemplating her response. She knew that revealing the identity of the source could jeopardize their safety and the integrity of the evidence. After careful consideration, she decided to share only what was necessary.

Riya replied "I understand your concern, Siddharth, her voice measured. "Vidya has been cautious in protecting the identity of the source to ensure their safety. We have verified the authenticity of the documents to the best of our abilities, and they seem to align with the information we already had. If you want you too should verified from your sources. However, the identity of the source remains confidential for now."

Siddharth nodded, understanding the need for discretion. "I trust your judgment, Riya," he said, his voice filled with conviction. "We must focus on corroborating the evidence and ensuring its admissibility in court. We need to work fast with the legal team and establish a solid foundation to present these findings effectively."

Riya asked Siddharth about the source of his information. Siddharth took a pause and requested Riya to listen to him carefully before reacting. Taking a seat, Riya anxiously awaited Siddharth's explanation, her mind filled with worry and anticipation. Siddharth took a deep breath and looked directly into Riya's eyes. "Riya, there's something I need to share with you. The mysterious man you encountered, the one you knew as Rohan, is the same person you knew as Raj, my school friend, he gather the evidence for us. He approached me with the information last night but with conditions"

Riya's eyes widened in surprise and confusion. "Raj? But I thought he had disappeared from my life. What does he have to do with all of this?" and now Rohan , what's is happening"? I'm confused" and "conditions" on what basis, said Riya angrily.

Siddharth said "Riya, I know this is overwhelming, but we need to stay calm and focused," trying to ease her anger. "Raj and Rohan are the same person. He has been operating under different identities to manipulate the situation and protect Parminder and more which I don't understand right now. Raj or Rohan, has crucial information that can help Parminder's case, but he has his terms".

Siddharth continued, "Rohan approached me, offering evidence that could potentially help Parminder's case. However, he had a condition. In exchange for providing the evidence and ensuring Parminder's freedom, he requested the identity of a person to be revealed and put in jail. This person would take the blame for the crimes, even though they were innocent." Rohan found himself in a difficult situation as he couldn't reveal the name of the powerful person involved in framing Parminder. This person had malicious intentions, seeking revenge for Parminder's refusal to be a part of their illegal activities. Despite being offered absurd and illegal deals, Parminder had chosen to sign with another party, which only fuelled the vengeful motives. With substantial evidence in hand, Rohan believed that this was a critical opportunity to save Parminder from the false accusations. However, revealing the powerful person's name would put not only Parminder but also himself and others at risk. He knew that handling the situation delicately was essential to ensure the safety and well-being of everyone involved."

Riya's mind was racing, trying to grasp the complexity of the situation. "So, Rohan wants to save Parminder at the expense of an innocent person? That's not right, Siddharth. We can't let someone else suffer for the crimes they didn't commit." Siddharth nodded, understanding

Riya's moral standpoint. "I agree, Riya. It's an unfair proposition, and justice must prevail. We cannot let an innocent person take the blame for Parminder's actions."

Riya's determination grew stronger as she realized the depth of the predicament. "We need to find a way to bring Rohan's true intentions to light and ensure Parminder's case is resolved fairly and justly. We can't let an innocent person be sacrificed for the sake of money and a settlement outside the court."

Siddharth agreed, "You're right, Riya. We need to investigate further, gather all the evidence, and expose the truth. It won't be easy, but we owe it to Parminder and to the principles of justice."

Siddharth took a deep breath and continued, "There's another condition Rohan has put forward, Riya. He insists on meeting you in person before providing all the evidence. He believes it's crucial for you to hear his side of the story directly."

Riya's mind was swirling with a mix of emotions. Meeting Rohan/Raj meant revisiting a part of her past that she had tried to move on from. As she tried to grasp the complexity of the situation. "So, Rohan wants me to meet him and settle things outside the court," she reasoned. "But why would he implicate an innocent person? This doesn't make sense."

Siddharth nodded and continued, "Raj/Rohan is willing to sacrifice an innocent person to protect his brother. He believes that person's involvement will divert attention from Parminder's case and ensure his brother's release. It's a dangerous game he's playing, and we need to be careful."

Riya felt a mix of emotions—anger, confusion, and a

sense of responsibility. "What should we do, Siddharth? How do we handle this?" she asked, searching for guidance.

"I've one more thing to add Riya, I've accepted Rohan both the demands". Riya was taken aback by Siddharth's revelation. Accepting Rohan's terms seemed like a risky move to her,"

"Siddharth, I do not understand you, why have you accepted Rohan's terms," Riya said, her voice laced with concern.

Siddharth with a assured voice. "I assure you, Riya, I haven't forgotten our pursuit of justice. Meeting Rohan will provide us with an opportunity to delve deeper into his intentions and gather more evidence. He is willing to talk to you and only you. We need to uncover the truth and protect Parminder, no matter what."

Riya looked into Siddharth's eyes, searching for the determination she had come to rely on. She knew that they shared the same goal, even if their methods differed. With a newfound resolve, she said, "Alright, Siddharth. Let's meet Rohan and find out what he has to say. But remember, we won't compromise our principles or let him control the narrative. We must stay focused on the truth."

Siddharth's face softened, and he nodded in agreement. "Riya, I appreciate your strength and conviction. I'm convince that together we will figure it out. I must say you have made the right decision, and I understand how difficult and painful it will be for you. But rest assured, your efforts won't go to waste."

After Siddharth left Riya felt void and lost. Riya's hands trembled as she dialled Vidya's number, her heart heavy with the weight of the revelations she had just experienced. After a few rings, Vidya answered the call, her voice filled with curiosity.

"Vidya, we need to meet," Riya said, her voice choked with emotion. "I have something important to tell you."

Vidya, sensing the urgency in Riya's tone, agreed to meet at their favourite café. As they sat face to face, Riya couldn't contain her emotions any longer. Tears streamed down her cheeks as she recounted the shocking truth about Rohan and Raj, how they were one and the same. Vidya listened intently, her expression shifting from surprise to disbelief. She reached out and held Riya's trembling hands, offering comfort and support. The weight of the revelation was heavy, and both friends struggled to process the magnitude of the situation. As Vidya also knows Rohan as a friend, she couldn't believe how she too missed such an important piece of information.

"I can't believe it, Riya," Vidya said, her voice filled with a mix of shock and concern. "How could Rohan, someone we knew, be involved in all of this? And Raj, his connection to it all... It's unimaginable. I know him from so long as a friend but this is unreal."

Riya nodded, tears still streaming down her face. She looked at Vidya and said, "Why my brother, he is innocent and he is been suffering from months now."

Vidya asked, "Riya, did you ever discuss Rohan with Parminder bhai?" Vidya's words struck a chord with Riya, making her realize that there were still unanswered questions that needed to be addressed. She felt a mix of regret and frustration for not having thought about it earlier. How could she have overlooked such an important aspect?

"You're right, Vidya," Riya admitted, her voice tinged with

self-disappointment. "I should have asked Parminder bhai about Rohan. And I need to have a conversation with Siddharth as well. I can't ignore the fact that Raj/Rohan have deceived me."

Vidya nodded in agreement, her concern for Riya evident in her eyes. "It's crucial to gather all the information and understand the truth behind their actions. We can't let ourselves be blinded by emotions or continue to be taken advantage of."

Riya took a deep breath, gathering her thoughts and steeling herself for the upcoming conversations. "You're right, Vidya. I need to confront the truth head-on, no matter how difficult it may be. I won't allow myself to be manipulated any longer. We need to uncover the truth, understand what's happening, and why all of this happened in the first place."

With newfound determination, Riya decided to have an honest conversation with Parminder, her brother, to shed light on the connection between Rohan and him. She needed to understand the dynamics of their relationship and why they had kept it a secret from her. Additionally, she planned to approach Siddharth and have a candid discussion about his knowledge of Rohan's true identity and involvement. It was crucial for Riya to ascertain Siddharth's intentions and ensure she wasn't being manipulated by those she trusted. Lastly, she has to meet Rohan and that thought itself was painful. But she has too she thought to her herself. She took the difficult path first. She decided to meet Rohan first. Riya gathered her courage and decided to confront Raj, also known as Rohan, before the upcoming hearing. She called him and requested a meeting, wanting to have a direct conversation about the revelations she had recently discovered. Rohan agreed, and they arranged to meet at a quiet café in the city.

As Riya entered the café, she noticed Rohan sitting at a corner table, his face masked with a mix of anticipation and apprehension. She took a deep breath, reminding herself to stay composed and assertive throughout the conversation. Walking up to the table, she greeted him with a cautious smile. "Raj cum Rohan, thank you for meeting me," Riya began, her voice tinged with a blend of determination and vulnerability. "I've learned a lot recently, and I need to discuss some important matters with you. "But before that, what should I address or call you as, Raj or Rohan?" Riya asked with a curious smile.

Raj chuckled warmly, "You can call me Rohan, Riya. It feels more familiar and comfortable that way."

"Alright, Rohan it is," Riya replied, Rohan nodded, his eyes reflecting a mixture of regret and remorse. "I understand, Riya. I owe you an explanation, and I'm prepared to face the consequences of my actions."

Riya took a seat opposite Rohan, her gaze fixed on him. "I now know that you and Raj are the same person. Why did you deceive me? Why did you choose to hide this from me?"

Rohan sighed, his voice filled with regret. "Riya, I didn't want to involve you in the mess I found myself in. I thought I could protect you by keeping my true identity hidden. It was a misguided attempt to shield you from the truth."

Riya's emotions were in turmoil as she listened to Rohan's explanation. The realization that he had been leading a double life and hiding his true identity from her was difficult to comprehend. She struggled to find the right words to express her feelings of betrayal and confusion. "Rohan, I can't believe you kept this from me for so long," Riya said, her voice trembling with a mix of anger and sadness. "You had the chance to be honest with me, to trust me with the truth. But instead, you chose to deceive me and involve yourself in this mess."

Rohan's eyes welled up with tears, his voice choked with emotion. "Riya, please understand that I never intended to hurt you. When I met you as Raj on social media, I saw a different side of you, a side that I fell in love with. I wanted to have a genuine connection with you, away from the facade of Rohan. But circumstances forced me to keep my true identity hidden."

Riya's eyes narrowed, her voice laced with frustration. "But that doesn't justify lying to me, Rohan. I trusted you, and you betrayed that trust. I deserve to know the whole truth." And giving way to a glimmer of understanding. "You mentioned that Siddharth was involved, that you shared everything with him. Why did you go to him instead of coming to me?"

Rohan: "I knew that Siddharth had connections and resources that could help us navigate this situation. I wanted to find a way to protect you and your family without causing further harm. I thought involving Siddharth was the best course of action."

Riya's voice trembled as she spoke, her eyes filled with pain." But what about me, Rohan? What about my feelings and my right to know the truth? I trusted you, and now I question everything. It's not just about the consequences; it's about the betrayal of my trust."

Rohan looked down, gathering his thoughts. "You're right, Riya. I should have been honest with you from the beginning. The truth is, I was blackmailed into helping Siddharth with evidence against those powerful individuals you mentioned. It was the only leverage I had to protect Parminder." Riya's eyes widened, a mix of surprise and concern washing over her. "So, you made a deal with Siddharth to expose those corrupt individuals in exchange for Parminder's freedom?"

Rohan nodded, his expression somber. "Yes, that was the agreement. But I never anticipated the consequences of my actions, especially the innocent person who would be implicated. I'm filled with guilt for what I've done." Riya's anger began to subside, replaced by a sense of empathy. She could see the torment in Rohan's eyes, and despite the betrayal, she understood the desperation he must have felt to save his brother.

"I won't condone what you've done, Rohan," Riya said firmly. "But if we're going to make things right, we need to ensure that innocent people aren't unjustly accused. We have to find a way to rectify the situation."

Rohan nodded, his voice filled with remorse. "I agree, Riya. I'm ready to cooperate fully and provide all the evidence I have. It's the least I can do to set things right."

Riya leaned forward, her eyes searching Rohan's face for answers. "Tell me more about this new deal and the powerful person's offer. I need to understand everything if we are going to find a way to save Parminder bhai," she said earnestly.

Rohan nodded, taking a moment to collect his thoughts. "The new deal was a significant opportunity for our business, but it came with a catch," he began. "The powerful person behind made an offer that seems too good to be true. They promised to secure the deal for us, but in return, they demanded a substantial cut of the profits. The catch is that deal involves some shady, possibly illegal practices."

His voice faltered, revealing the weight of the situation. "Parminder refused their offer, knowing the consequences of getting involved with such a person. He chose to pursue an honest path, signing the deal with another party. That's when the trouble started. It seems this powerful person is now trying to frame Parminder to destroy his reputation and business."

Riya's eyes widened with concern as she absorbed the gravity of the situation. "So, this person is retaliating because Parminder didn't go along with their plan?" she asked.

"Yes, exactly," Rohan confirmed. "And now, they are using all their influence and resources to paint a false picture, making Parminder look guilty of things he didn't do. It's a ruthless game they are playing, and we need to be careful."

Riya's mind raced with possibilities. "Is there any evidence to prove Parminder's innocence? Can we counter their false claims?"

Rohan sighed, his face tense with worry. "We are working on gathering evidence, but it's not easy. This person is well-connected and has people in their pocket. But I believe in Parminder's innocence, and I won't stop fighting until we clear his name." Trust me this time".

Rohan reached out, trying to touch Riya's hand, but she pulled away. "I never wanted to hurt you, Riya. You have to believe that. Yes, I made mistakes, but I was torn between my loyalty to Parminder and my growing feelings for you. It's not an excuse, but I need you to understand the struggle I faced."

Riya's voice quivered with a mix of sadness and frustration. "You say you love me, but love doesn't justify deception. I need time to process everything and figure out what this means for us. Right now, I can't forgive you."

Rohan nodded, tears streaming down his face. "I understand, Riya. I never wanted to cause you pain. I will respect your need for space and time. Just know that I will do whatever it takes to make things right, even if it means disappearing from your life again." With those words, Rohan stood up, his heart heavy with regret and sorrow. He left the café, not knowing what the future held for him or for his relationship with Riya. It was a painful realization that love alone wasn't enough to undo the damage caused by lies and secrets. Both Riya and Rohan would have to face the consequences of their choices and find a way to heal, either together or separately.

Riya understood that she needed time to heal from the emotional turmoil that had consumed her. The weight of the revelations and the betrayal she had experienced had taken a toll on her heart and mind. She realized that rushing into any decisions or judgments would not be beneficial for her well-being. She learned valuable lessons about trust, honesty, and the complexities of human relationships. Riya understood that her journey of healing was a personal one, and she refused to let the actions of others define her worth or her future.

Riya decided to give herself some time to heal and come out of the pain she was experiencing near her chest. Then she decided to meet her brother Parminder. With a heavy heart, Riya mustered up the courage to meet her brother, Parminder, amidst the turmoil that had engulfed their lives. She understood that their relationship had been deeply affected by the revelations and the involvement of both Parminder and Rohan in the scandal. Riya approached the meeting with a mix of emotions—anger, hurt, and a desire for answers. She knew that confronting Parminder would not be easy, but she needed to understand his motivations and confront the reality of their shared involvement.

As they sat face to face, Riya could see the guilt and remorse etched on Parminder's face. The weight of his actions and the consequences they had brought upon their family were evident. It was a somber and emotional atmosphere, with unspoken words lingering in the air. She took a moment to gather her thoughts, her voice filled with a mix of disappointment and concern. "Bhai, I understand that you wanted to make our father proud and protect our family. But what you failed to realize is that the means you chose to achieve that went against everything we were taught. The path of greed, deceit, and hiding the truth only leads to destruction, not success."

Parminder nodded, acknowledging his mistake. "I know, sis. I made a grave error in judgment, and I regret it deeply. I was blinded by my ambition and greed. But I didn't cheat anyone. I couldn't see the consequences of my actions. I trusted someone without consulting my business partner for the sake of quick progress and big money.

Riya's voice softened as she saw the remorse in Parminder's eyes. "Bhai, I understand that you were driven by good intentions, but that doesn't excuse the choices you made. You should have involved and discussed this with father and your business partner before making such a huge decision. We are responsible for our actions, and we must face the consequences. Our family's reputation has been tarnished, and it will take time and effort to rebuild the trust that has been shattered."

Parminder sighed, his voice filled with regret. "I know, Riya. I wish I could turn back time and undo all the damage I've caused. But I promise you, I will do everything in my power to make amends. I will cooperate with the authorities, take full responsibility for my actions, and work towards rebuilding our family's name."

Riya looked at her brother, tears welling up in her eyes. "Bhai, I want to believe you. I want to see the brother I knew, the one who cared for our family's well-being above all else.

Parminder reached out and held Riya's hand, his grip firm yet filled with remorse. "Sis, I understand that rebuilding trust won't happen overnight. I will do whatever it takes to earn back trust and prove that I am committed to changing for the better.

Riya nodded, her voice filled with a mixture of sadness and hope. "Bhai, I want nothing more than for our family to heal and move forward. I appreciate your honesty and willingness to accept your mistake, but it's important to remember that decisions like these should be made together, as a family."

She reached out and placed her hand on Parminder's, offering a gesture of comfort. "We all make mistakes, Bhai. What's important is that we learn from them and strive to make things right. I can sense your remorse, and I believe that you genuinely want to rectify the situation."

Parminder nodded, his gaze filled with gratitude. "Thank you, sis, for understanding. I know that understanding alone won't undo the pain and consequences caused, but it means a lot to me. I am truly sorry for not involving you and father and my business partner in the decision-making process and for trusting only my judgment for quick success. I can see now that I made a mistake. "

Riya smiled softly, a glimmer of forgiveness in her eyes. "Bhai, we're all human, and we're bound to make mistakes. What matters now is how we move forward.

Parminder: Riya, there's something I need to confess. It's been weighing heavily on my heart. I'm filled with guilt for what I did, for stopping Rohan from meeting you. I want you to know that it wasn't his fault or decision. He genuinely likes you.

Riya: (Taken aback) What do you mean, Bhai? But why..? Why did you prevent him from meeting me?

Parminder: Riya, please understand that I had good intentions. After getting to know Rohan's circle and business associations, I felt he wouldn't be the right person for you. I wanted to protect you, our family, and your reputation. I made the decision as your brother, without consulting you or considering your feelings. I realize now that my judgment was misled and wrong.

Riya: (Feeling a mix of emotions) Bhai, I appreciate that you were trying to protect me and our family. But how could you make such a decision without involving me? It's my life, and my happiness should also be considered. Did you not trust my judgment or believe that I could make the right choice for myself?

Parminder: Riya, I deeply regret not involving you in that decision. I was blinded by my concerns and failed to see the impact it would have on you. I didn't trust your judgment, and for that, I am truly sorry. I never wanted to hurt you or undermine your ability to make decisions for yourself.

Riya: (Feeling hurt but also wanting to find a way forward) Bhai, it's difficult for me to understand how you didn't trust me enough to make my own choices. It made me doubt myself and question my own feelings. I need you to know that I am capable of making decisions for my own life.

Parminder: Riya, I understand and I can see the pain it has caused. I should have had more faith in you. I'm truly sorry for putting you through this. I want to make this right for all of us and rebuild the trust between us and support you in making your own choices.

Riya: (Taking a deep breath) Bhai, trust and open communication are essential in relationship. I need to know that you value my opinions and respect my autonomy. Moving forward, let's promise each other that we'll make decisions together, with both our perspectives in mind.

Parminder: (Regretful but determined) Riya, I promise to learn from my mistake and involve you in decisions that directly affect your life. I want to foster a stronger bond based on trust and open communication. You deserve to have a say in your own happiness, and I will do my best to support you.

Riya: Bhai, I just spoke with Rohan, and he didn't mention anything about you stopping him from meeting me. I'm a little confused now. Can you explain?

Parminder: Riya, I understand your confusion. I didn't communicate this to Rohan directly, but he understood my concerns about him being with you. He respected my opinion and decided not to pursue a relationship with you. I have come to realize that I misjudged him based on his work and circle. He genuinely likes you and was willing to step aside to protect both of us and our family.

Riya: (Surprised and thoughtful) So, Rohan knew about your concerns and doubts, yet he chose to respect your wishes. That shows a lot about his character and his commitment to our well-being. I'm starting to see him in a different light now.

Parminder: Yes, Riya. Rohan's actions have made me respect him more as well. He prioritized our family's reputation and didn't want to come between us. I regret not giving him a chance earlier and misjudging him solely based on his background.

Riya: (Reflective) It's a valuable lesson for me too, Bhai. I realize now that judging someone solely on their work and associations may not give the full picture of who they truly are. I appreciate Rohan's understanding and respect for our family.

Parminder: Riya, I'm glad we're on the same page now. It's important for us to recognize our mistakes and learn from them. Rohan has shown us that he cares about us and has good intentions. We should give him the chance he deserves.

Riya: You're right, Bhai. I don't want to let my previous judgments cloud my perception of Rohan anymore. I want to approach this with an open mind and see where things go. Thank you for being honest with me and helping me understand the situation better. The conversation between Riya and Parminder brought clarity and understanding, also brought their feelings and perspectives to the surface. They also discuss about that new deal and about the powerful person offer. As their conversation concluded, Riya and Parminder embraced the opportunity for growth and understanding. They acknowledged their past mistakes, sought forgiveness, and committed to building a stronger sibling bond based on trust, respect, and shared decision-making.

Riya, feeling a renewed sense of strength and clarity, decided to reach out to Siddharth to discuss the situation and seek his views and opinions. She believed his perspective would be crucial in helping her navigate the complexities of her relationship with Rohan and her family.

Riya: Siddharth, I hope you're available to talk. There's something important I need to discuss with you.

Siddharth: Of course, Riya. I'm here for you. What's on your mind?

Riya: I've had some significant revelations recently regarding Parminder and Rohan. I've learned that Parminder had stopped Rohan from meeting me, thinking it was for the best. However, I've come to realize that I misjudged Rohan based on his background and associations. Now, I'm torn between my feelings for Rohan and my family's concerns. I value your opinion and need your guidance on this matter.

Siddharth: I appreciate your trust in me, Riya. It's essential to consider both your heart and your family's concerns in a situation like this. I've known Rohan for a long time, and I can attest to his character and integrity. He genuinely cares about you and your family's well-being. While it's natural for your family to be protective, it's important to weigh their concerns against your own judgment and feelings.

Riya: That's precisely what I've been struggling with, Siddharth. I want to honour my family's wishes, but I also don't want to dismiss my own emotions and the connection I share with Rohan. It's challenging to find the right balance.

Siddharth: It's a delicate balance indeed, Riya. Remember that your happiness and well-being should also be considered. Open communication and understanding between you, Rohan, and your family will be crucial moving forward. Perhaps you can have a heartfelt conversation with your family, expressing your feelings and assuring them that you will handle the situation responsibly.

Riya: You're right, Siddharth. Communication is key. I need to have an open and honest dialogue with my family, ensuring them that I will make informed decisions and prioritize both my happiness and our family's goodwill. Thank you for your guidance. It means a lot to me.

Siddharth: You're welcome, Riya. I believe in you, and I'm here to support you through this journey. Take your time, have those conversations, and trust your instincts. Remember, love and understanding can bridge even the most challenging situations.

Riya, still feeling confused and hurt, expressed her concerns to Siddharth, "You knew your friend well, and I'm sure you never had any problem with him. You were meeting him and discussing everything with him, but you never once mentioned him to me. Why did you do this to me? I was so open and transparent about my feelings and my family, and yet you kept this from me. Our family treated you like a member, and you knew I was waiting for someone special?"

Siddharth: Riya, you need to trust me. I accepted that deal to ensure that you and your family wouldn't be hurt. I do know Rohan, but I had no idea about your feelings for him until you told me recently. In our line of work, we deal with legal proceedings and complex situations every day. Our focus is to find evidence and fight for our clients. It's not personal; it's about doing our job. Right now, we need to consider taking the offer and finding a way to protect Rohan as well. Trust me and my team. We will do our best. Your brother will be out soon, and you can go home to your family. I know how much they mean to you.

Riya (sadly): What about us, Siddharth? Did we have any moments between us?

Long pause

Riya held the phone in her hand, waiting for Siddharth's response, but there was no answer from the other end.

The silence stretched on, intensifying the uncertainty and leaving Riya feeling even more disheartened. It seemed as though the question she had posed hung in the air, unanswered, adding to the emotional distance between them. Riya's emotions were overwhelming, and in that moment, she needed time and space to process everything that had happened. Siddharth's explanation left her conflicted, unsure of how to reconcile her feelings for Rohan and her trust in Siddharth. She needed time alone to reflect on her own desires and priorities before engaging in further conversation.

Riya, filled with a mix of emotions, decided to call her parents in the midst of all the confusion. She wanted to update them about the information and evidence they had collected. She dialled their number, and her father answered, listening attentively to her words. He motioned for her mother to join the conversation, indicating the importance of what Riya had to say.

Father: "Riya, my child, let us hear everything."
Riya proceeded to explain everything, sharing the details and developments with her parents. After hearing her out, her father responded with advice that carried wisdom and perspective.

Father: "It's karma, Riya. You mustn't judge anyone. Let the truth prevail. Truth is not always black or white; there are shades of gray as well. Accept that your brother's ambition to grow and innocence have led him to where he is, and he is facing the consequences. As for Rohan, he too will experience his share of hurt and pain. He should have told you the truth, but he confided in Siddharth instead. It is because of his truth and courage that your brother can be free. Rohan realized that he couldn't stay silent or give up, and he did what he thought was right. On the other hand, Siddharth played a crucial role in bringing everything together. It is destiny and Siddharth's fate to bring justice for all. He stood by his friend and waited for the right moment to inform you. Even Rohan supported his friend and didn't question Parminder's decision to proceed with the deal and cut off contact with you. Everyone played their part, and from their perspective, they may not be entirely wrong, but not fully right either."

Father continued: "Riya, I'm sorry that you have to go through all of this, but I am proud of you for not being biased and for being able to see things clearly. Life is not always black and white as we imagine and desire it to be. Sometimes, life teaches us to see things differently and not hastily pass judgments. Try to understand each other's perspectives and give each other a chance. Everyone deserves a second chance. I urged not punish, accept, and move on."

Riya sought clarification from her father, questioning why it had to be her who faced these challenges.
Riya: "So, Father, why me?"
Father: "Think, why not you? Only you possess the courage and wisdom to see things clearly and the strength to forgive and understand. Who else but you? Life is teaching you the lessons you need to learn for your better future. Everything happens for a reason."
Father: "Let Siddharth produce the evidence in court. He knows the law and its consequences."
Father: "Let Rohan find more evidence and save innocent person."
In closing, her father encouraged Riya to stand with Siddharth and bring back their son, her brother.
Father: "Riya, stand with Siddharth and bring back my son, my child. Come back home!
Riya: "Yes Father"

EIGHT
A New Beginning

Nov 2010

On the final day, the courtroom was filled with parents, friends, and other family members, anxiously awaiting the proceedings. Siddharth and his team stood prepared, armed with the evidence they had diligently gathered. Although a slight nervousness could be seen on their faces, they maintained their composure. Rohan, unable to meet the gaze of Riya or her parents, stood in the courtroom, carrying the weight of his actions. Riya and her family and Vidya sat behind Siddharth and his team, her anticipation palpable as she awaited the arrival of the judge.

The atmosphere in the courtroom was tense as everyone awaited the final verdict. The judge, clad in a black robe, entered the room and took their seat on the bench. The silence was deafening as the judge prepared to deliver their decision. After carefully reviewing the evidence presented by Siddharth and his team, the judge began to speak. They meticulously analyzed the facts and testimonies, ensuring a fair judgment. The tension in the room reached its peak as the judge's words hung in the air.

Finally, the judge pronounced their verdict. They declared Parminder not guilty, relieving him of all charges. A wave of relief washed over the family and friends who had been holding their breath, their worry finally dissipating. Tears of joy streamed down the faces of Riya's parents, a sense of justice prevailing. Simultaneously, the judge addressed the person who had falsely taken the blame, cautioning them about their actions and granting them release. However, the court did not stop there. They ordered further investigations into the bank and shell company dealings, demanding the arrest of those involved. Siddharth and his team accepted the responsibility bestowed upon them with determination and pride. They vowed to pursue the truth with firm dedication, assuring the court that they would leave no stone unturned in their pursuit of justice. There was only one shortfall that Siddharth and his team failed to trace the disappeared funds from Parminder's account. Despite their tireless efforts, the source of the missing money remained elusive, leaving a significant hole in the financial scenario of the Malhotra family.

As the proceedings concluded, Riya's parents embraced each other and their daughter, overwhelmed with relief and gratitude. The journey had been arduous, but justice had prevailed, thanks to the relentless efforts of Siddharth, his team, and the support of their loved ones.

Riya's parents couldn't express their gratitude enough to Vidya, Siddharth and his team. Filled with overwhelming emotions, Riya's father approached Parminder, his eyes welling up with tears. He tightly embraced his son, holding him close, feeling a mix of relief and forgiveness. Parminder, realizing the depth of his actions, humbly touched his father's feet, seeking forgiveness for the pain he had caused.

Riya's mother, filled with a sense of peace, wrapped her arms around her son, cherishing the moment of reconciliation and restoration. The weight of the past seemed to lift off her shoulders, replaced by a renewed sense of love and togetherness.

Meanwhile, Riya stood by Siddharth and his team, congratulating them on their remarkable efforts and dedication. She couldn't help but feel immense pride for the man she had come to rely on throughout the challenging journey. The bond between Riya and Siddharth had grown stronger, their shared experiences forging an unbreakable connection.

Riya's father, with a proud smile on his face, approached Rohan. He extended his hand in a gesture of gratitude and appreciation. In that moment, he acknowledged Rohan's unshakeable support and understanding. Filled with admiration, Riya's father invited Rohan to Delhi, extending an open invitation to their home. Rohan was taken aback by the unexpected invitation but also felt a glimmer of hope. He saw it as an opportunity to make amends, not just with Riya, but also with her family. With a grateful nod, he replied, "Thank you, sir. I appreciate your invitation. I would be honoured to visit Delhi and have a chance to speak with you and your family."

Rohan's acceptance of the invitation signalled his willingness to face the consequences of his actions and seek redemption. He understood that this trip to Delhi was not just about physical distance but also about bridging the emotional gap he had created. He was ready to confront his mistakes, express his remorse, and show his genuine desire to change. Riya's father smiled warmly, acknowledging Rohan's acceptance. He recognized the sincerity in Rohan's words and hoped that this journey would lead to healing and understanding for all parties involved.

Vidya, overwhelmed with emotions, approached Siddharth and team to express her gratitude and admiration. She commended their tireless dedication and the relentless pursuit of justice. Vidya understood the significance of their work in bringing the truth to light and ensuring Parminder's innocence. Siddharth also expressed his respect for Vidya's immense contribution, trust, and unwavering support to Riya's family. After expressing her appreciation to Siddharth and his team, Vidya also took a moment to briefly meet with Parminder and Rohan. With tears of relief and joy in her eyes, she hugged Parminder tightly, feeling a deep sense of relief that he had been vindicated. She thanked Rohan for his courage in speaking the truth, acknowledging that his honesty had played a crucial role in securing Parminder's release.

Rohan glanced towards Riya, hoping for even a small acknowledgment, he noticed that she didn't meet his gaze. Her eyes remained fixed on the ground, lost in a whirlwind of emotions and thoughts. The pain and confusion in her eyes were evident, but she chose not to respond to Rohan's glance, wanting to take time to process everything that had transpired. Meanwhile, Siddharth, understanding Riya's need for space, held her hand gently, providing a silent reassurance of his support. He spoke softly, "Riya, I respect your decision, whatever it may be. Take the time you need to sort through your feelings. Know that I trust you, and I'll be here for you, no matter what. Also I ensure you that our team will keep investigating and researching about the missing funds".

With those comforting words, Siddharth left the courtroom, accompanied by his team. The weight of the proceedings and the responsibility ahead were evident in his expression, but his determination remained unshakeable. As he walked towards his car, he knew that the journey for justice was far from over. He was committed to uncovering the complete truth and ensuring that those responsible faced the consequences of their actions.

As Rohan approached Riya, his heart filled with remorse and a deep longing for forgiveness. He mustered the courage to speak, "Riya, I am truly sorry for everything that has happened. I never intended to hurt you or your family. Can we meet again? Riya, still processing her emotions, looked at Rohan with a mix of sadness and a glimmer of forgiveness. However, she shook her head gently, indicating her unwillingness to meet at that moment. Without saying a word, she turned away, took vidya and joined her parents and other family members who were waiting to cheer and celebrate their hard-earned victory in the courtroom. The atmosphere was filled with relief and joy as Riya's parents, along with their loved ones, embraced each other, expressing their gratitude and appreciation for the successful outcome. They felt a renewed sense of hope and unity, having come through a challenging ordeal together.

Rohan stood there, watching Riya leave with her family, understanding the weight of his actions and the consequences they had on their relationship. He knew that the road to redemption would not be easy, but he remained hopeful that someday he would have the opportunity to make amends and seek forgiveness.

Next day morning Riya returned to Delhi with her parents, she couldn't shake off the lingering confusion and hurt that plagued her heart. Uncertain about her next steps, she felt that spending time with her parents might bring some solace and clarity. Wanting to take some time to reflect and heal, she made the decision to inform Siddharth that she would be taking a break for a few weeks and send message to Siddharth.

Riya: (typing) Hey Siddharth, I hope you're doing well. I wanted to send you a quick message while I'm on the plane. I just wanted to say thank you once again for everything you've done for me and my family. Your strength and support have been invaluable throughout this whole journey. As I head back to Delhi with my parents, I'm still processing everything that has happened. This break will give me the opportunity to reflect on my feelings and find my own path forward. I want you to know that this break doesn't change how I feel about you or our connection. I believe that time and distance will bring clarity, and I hope to come to a better understanding of my own heart. I appreciate your patience and understanding during this time. Please take care of yourself and know that you're always in my thoughts. I'll be in touch soon. Until then, stay strong and keep fighting for justice.

Sending you warm wishes, Riya

2 and half year later....

Over the course of two and a half years, Riya, Siddharth, Rohan, and Vidya had embarked on a transformative journey that brought about remarkable changes in their lives. The events that unfolded during this period had shaped their perspectives, aspirations, and relationships in profound ways. Each individual had embarked on their own unique journey, navigating the complexities of life and embracing the opportunities that came their way. Their collective story unfolded with a touch of realism, capturing the essence of their growth and the intricacies of their relationships.

Riya, driven by her passion and expertise, had seamlessly integrated herself into her father's business. Embracing her role with determination and vision, she embarked on an exciting venture, spearheading a new division focused on the realm of export and import. Through her innovative strategies and dedication, she breathed new life into the business, propelling it towards unexplored heights. Meanwhile, Parminder, having found love and started his own family, embraced the joys and responsibilities of marriage and fatherhood. After weathering the storm that had threatened to dismantle their family's legacy, Riya and Parminder emerged stronger than ever, their trust in each other reignited and their determination remain strong and firm.

Together, Riya and Parminder embarked on a transformative journey, challenging conventional norms and embracing innovation. With complementary skills and unwavering commitment, they propelled the company towards new horizons. Adapting to the dynamic market, they devised a strategic plan, leveraging Riya's expertise in international trade and Parminder's business acumen. The result was exponential growth and success. Fuelled by their shared passion and a deep-rooted sense of responsibility, Riya and Parminder implemented bold initiatives. They expanded the company's reach into new international markets, forged strategic partnerships, and fostered a culture of creativity and collaboration.

Through relentless effort, they transformed the company into one of the top exporters of authentic Indian garments and designer outfits to the global market. The production doubled, and strategic partnerships flourished both nationally and internationally. Their success turned them into iconic business figures, representing Indian culture and ethics. The company's growth was unprecedented, leading to the opening of multiple showrooms across India through strategic partnerships. Riya and Parminder's unwavering vision and dedication had not only secured their family's legacy but also positioned them as prominent leaders in the fashion industry, symbolizing the rich heritage of India on a global stage.

Their parents, witnessing the remarkable evolution of their children, made a conscious decision to step back from the daily operations of the business. Filled with pride and confidence in their children's abilities, they entrusted the reins of the family enterprise to Riya and Parminder. With a newfound freedom, the parents embraced a well-deserved break, cherishing the opportunity to explore their own passions and relish the simple joys of life. Their support and guidance continued to serve as a pillar of strength for Riya and Parminder, fuelling their determination to carry the family legacy forward. This act of trust and support not only solidified the family bond but also served as a testament to the growth and maturity of the siblings.

Amidst their professional pursuits, Riya, Siddharth, Rohan, and Vidya remained deeply connected as friends. They celebrated each other's successes, provided a shoulder to lean on during challenging times, and shared the journey of personal growth together. Their bond served as a constant source of strength, reminding them of the importance of friendship and support in navigating life's twists and turns.

While Siddharth remained committed to his job, he also played an integral role in the growth of the new division that he and Riya had established in international business and trade. Leveraging his expertise and experience, Siddharth brought a unique perspective to the table, navigating the complexities of the global market and forging strategic alliances. His dedication and knowledge propelled the division to new heights, contributing to the overall success of the family business.

As the journey continued, Siddharth found himself immersed in his role of seeking justice and fighting against the fraudulent shell company. Together with his trusted friend, Rohan, they tirelessly pursued the truth, unearthing the intricate web of deceit and exposing those responsible. Their shared determination to bring the perpetrators to justice strengthened their friendship and bond, as they supported each other through the challenges they faced.

In addition to their professional collaborations, Siddharth and Rohan maintained a strong friendship outside of work. They regularly met, not only to discuss business matters but also to share laughs, reminisce about old times, and provide each other with support. Their bond transcended their professional endeavour's, serving as a constant reminder of the importance of genuine connections and the strength that friendship brings.

As Rohan's journey unfolded, he embarked on a new entrepreneurial venture driven by a fresh set of values and a clear agenda. Guided by his experiences and the support of Siddharth, he set out to create a business that aligned with his own principles and vision. With a strong belief in ethical practices and social responsibility, Rohan assembled a team of like-minded individuals who shared his passion for making a positive impact. These new alliances provided a solid foundation for Rohan's business, enabling him to expand his reach and influence.

With his new team in place, Rohan fostered a work environment that prioritized transparency, integrity, and collaboration. He nurtured a culture where each team member's voice was heard, encouraging innovation and creative problem-solving. Through his leadership, Rohan inspired his team to embrace their individual strengths and work collectively towards a shared purpose. Rohan's new venture not only brought financial success but also allowed him to make a difference in the lives of others. His commitment to social responsibility and giving back to the community became a cornerstone of his business. Whether through charitable initiatives, environmental sustainability efforts, or supporting local causes, Rohan ensured that his company's growth went hand in hand with making a positive impact on society.

Throughout his journey, Siddharth remained a trusted advisor and ally to Rohan. Their friendship and shared values continued to shape their professional collaborations, as they sought to create a better world through their respective endeavours. Together, they exemplified the power of partnerships and the potential for meaningful change when individuals come together with a common purpose.

While Vidya, the tenacious journalist, remained unwavering in her pursuit of truth and justice, she reached new heights in her career, leaving an indelible mark on the field of investigative journalism. Her relentless dedication and fearlessness led her to uncover a series of high-profile scandals and corruption cases, earning her accolades and recognition within the industry. Armed with her unyielding determination and a deep sense of responsibility towards society, Vidya fearlessly delved into the darkest corners of power, exposing the hidden truths and shedding light on the injustices that plagued the system. With unshakable integrity and an firm commitment to uncovering the truth, she became a beacon of hope for those who sought transparency and accountability.

Each ground breaking exposé further solidified Vidya's reputation as a journalist of immense integrity and uncompromising honesty. She fearlessly confronted the powerful, giving voice to the voiceless and standing up for the marginalized. Her work resonated with the public, sparking conversations and inspiring meaningful change. Amidst the acclaim and recognition, Vidya remained grounded and driven by her unshakeable mission to expose the truth and hold those in power accountable. Her firm commitment to investigative journalism became a symbol of hope and a source of inspiration for aspiring journalists and truth-seekers. Her fearless pursuit of justice became a rallying cry for those who believed in the power of the truth to transform lives and bring about meaningful change.

Vidya, celebrating her promotions, decides to throw a grand party and invites everyone, including Riya, Siddharth, and Rohan. The atmosphere is filled with joy and laughter as they reminisce about the past and enjoy the present moment. Throughout the night, Riya, Siddharth, Rohan, and Vidya share laughs, engage in lively conversations, and create beautiful memories together. The bond between them has grown stronger over time, and they cherish the friendship they have built.

As the party comes to an end, Riya embraces Vidya and Rohan, expressing her gratitude for their presence in her life. She bids them goodnight with a warm smile and suddenly lights dimmed and the room fell into silence, Riya felt a sense of anticipation wash over her. Suddenly, a spotlight illuminated her, casting a soft glow around her. Another spotlight revealed Siddharth standing behind her, his eyes filled with love and excitement. Riya's heart skipped a beat as she turned to face him, her eyes shimmering with emotion. Siddharth took a step closer, his voice filled with warmth and sincerity. "Riya," he began, his words carrying a depth of emotion, "From the moment I met you, my life has been filled with joy and love. You have become the light of my world, and I can't imagine a future without you by my side." He knelt down on one knee, holding a small box in his hand, and continued, "I've waited my whole life for someone like you, someone who completes me in every way. You have shown me what true love means, and I am certain that you are the one for me."

Opening the box, Siddharth revealed a beautiful ring, shimmering with elegance and grace. "Riya, will you do me the incredible honour of accompanying me on this journey called life? Will you be my partner, my confidante, and my best friend? Together, let's embark on an unknown path, where our love will create a beautiful life filled with endless possibilities."

Riya's heart swelled with overwhelming emotions as Siddharth knelt before her, holding out the ring. She felt a rush of gratitude for all the love and support he had showered upon her throughout their journey together. The depth of his belief in their love and his commitment to her touched her soul. With tear-filled eyes and a voice filled with sincerity, Riya spoke from the depths of her heart, "Siddharth, I am beyond grateful for the love you have poured into my life. You have made me feel cherished, supported, and understood in ways I never thought possible. Your belief in us, in our love, has given me strength and courage to face any challenge that comes our way."

She paused, taking a deep breath to gather her thoughts, wanting to convey the profound impact Siddharth had on her life. "You have seen me at my best and my worst, and yet you have loved me unconditionally. You have been my rock, my confidant, and my biggest supporter. I am in awe of your patience, your kindness, and the way you have always believed in me, even when I struggled to believe in myself."

Riya reached out, gently touching Siddharth's face, her voice filled with tenderness. "I never imagined that someone could love me as deeply and fiercely as you do. You have waited for me, understanding the importance of timing and giving me the space I needed. Your love has been patient and steadfast, and I am forever grateful."

She took a moment to let her words sink in, her gaze locked with Siddharth's. "So, with all my heart, I say 'yes.' Yes to this incredible journey we are about to embark on. Yes to a future filled with love, laughter, and shared dreams. Yes to facing challenges hand in hand, knowing that together we are stronger than ever."

Riya's voice trembled with a mixture of excitement and vulnerability as she continued, "I promise to love you fiercely and unconditionally, just as you have loved me. I promise to be there for you, to support you, and to cherish every moment we have together. You are my everything, Siddharth, and I am beyond grateful to have you as my partner for life." Siddharth's eyes gleamed with tears of joy as he embraced Riya, their hearts beating as one.

As the room filled with jubilant cheers and applause, Vidya's eyes sparkled with joy, seeing her dear friend Riya finding love and Siddharth as her partner. Overwhelmed by the moment, she embraced Riya tightly, expressing her heartfelt congratulations and best wishes. "Riya, my dear friend, I am so thrilled for you! Siddharth is an incredible partner, and I can see the love and happiness radiating from both of you. May your journey together be filled with boundless joy, support, and a love that grows stronger with each passing day."

Rohan, too, couldn't contain his happiness for Riya. He joined the embrace, enveloping both Riya and Siddharth in a warm hug. "Congratulations, Riya! Siddharth, you're a lucky man to have her by your side. May your love continue to flourish, and may you both find endless bliss and fulfilment in each other's arms. Cheers to a beautiful future together!"

Touched by the genuine love and support surrounding them, Riya and Siddharth shared a look of gratitude and contentment. They felt the immense joy of not only finding love but also having such incredible friends by their side. They embraced Vidya and Rohan once more, savouring the depth of their friendship and the beautiful moments they had shared.

In that moment of warmth and connection, the four friends understood the power of love, friendship, and the magic of life's precious bonds. Their hearts were filled with gratitude for the journey they had undertaken together, and the memories they would continue to create.

As they stood there, united in love and friendship, they knew that no matter what challenges or triumphs lay ahead, they would face them together, supporting and cheering each other on every step of the way. And with that, they raised a toast to love, to friendship, and to the incredible adventure that awaited them all.

About The Author

Preeti Khankhoje, is a serial entrepreneur turned author. As the Co-founder of Vivid Brand Communication, a renowned branding agency, Preeti has successfully navigated various industries throughout her incredible 25-year life journey. Her unwavering dedication to seeking answers to life's mysteries has been a lifelong pursuit.

With a strategic mindset and branding expertise, Preeti has spent the last two decades establishing and growing businesses with remarkable results. Her unconventional approach has earned her numerous accolades, while her firm, Vivid Brand Communication, is widely appreciated for its achievements under her visionary leadership.

In addition to her entrepreneurial ventures, Preeti has now expanded her creative pursuits as an author. Her fiction books delve into captivating stories, inviting readers to explore the depths of the human experience. With her insightful storytelling and profound understanding of people, Preeti brings her fictional worlds to life, offering a blend of entertainment, introspection, and inspiration.

Stay Connected

Instagram- https://instagram.com/khankhojepreeti/
Facebook- https://www.facebook.com/preeti.khankhoje/
LinkedIn- https://www.linkedin.com/in/preeti-khankhoje

Author Email: preetikhankhoje09@gmail.com

▷▷▷